For thirteen years now *Perry Rhodan* has been acknowledged to be the world's top-selling science fiction series. Originally published in magazine form in Germany, the series has now appeared in hardback and paperback in the States.

Over five hundred *Perry Rhodan* clubs exist on the Continent and *Perry Rhodan* fan conventions are held annually. The first *Perry Rhodan* film, 'SOS From Outer Space' has now been released in Europe.

The series has sold over *140 million* copies in Europe alone.

D1352350

Also available in the *Perry Rhodan* series

Clark Darlton

PERRY RHODAN 9

Quest Through Space and Time

Futura Publications Limited
An Orbit Book

An Orbit Book

First published in Great Britain in 1975
by Futura Publications Limited

Copyright © Ace Books 1971
An Ace Book, by arrangement with
Arthur Moewig Verlag

This series was created by Karl-Herbert Scheer and
Walter Ernsting. This edition translated by
Wendayne Ackerman and edited by Donald A. Wollheim.

ISBN 0 8600 7867 1

Printed in Great Britain by
Cox & Wyman Ltd,
London, Reading and Fakenham

Futura Publications Limited
110 Warner Road, London SE5

ORDER OF THE ACTION

1. THE CRYPT OF LIGHT

The Vega system.

Ferrol, eighth planet of the system, more than twenty-seven light-years from Earth.

And the Ferrons had concluded a trade treaty with Perry Rhodan, the representative of mankind. Friendly relations had been established between the two interstellar cultures. On the surface there was no compelling reason to delay any longer the great space expedition's return to home base.

If one regarded the whole problem from a purely technical point of view. But there were, of course, other considerations apart from the mere technical feasibility of a quick trip back to Terra, considerations which kept Perry Rhodan and his men on Ferrol.

Ferrol circled the Vega sun closer than Earth did Sol. As a consequence the Ferronian climate was much hotter than Terra's. The native population, a humanoid race, was well protected against the searing rays of their sun by a head of thick coppery hair and a bluish complexion. They were not much over five feet tall and their squat figures seemed an ideal adjustment to their home planet's gravity of 1.4–G's.

Coppery hair, blue skin, stocky body, tiny mouth, deep-set eyes – how insignificant if one looked at it from a cosmic viewpoint. Particularly insignificant to those individuals who comprehended the size and diversity of the worlds of our universe.

Such a one, for instance, as Reginald Bell.

The short, heavy-set Earthman, whose red bristles seemed always to stand on end, excitedly paced the floor in the control center of the giant spacesphere. A strange fire glowed in his pale-blue, almost faded eyes.

'We got a rotten deal from this positronic brain!' he growled. He punctuated his displeasure with wild flailing gestures of his great hands. 'Here we sit waiting for an answer from this brainy monster and I doubt that we'll ever hear from it. We've had it, Perry!'

The two men stood within the semicircle of the ship's control center. Rhodan, the leader of the expedition, was thirty-six, two years older than his friend Bell. Rhodan's lean figure revealed toughness and courage. Determination sparkled in his gray eyes – and a great sense of humor.

'Are you serious, Reg?' Rhodan looked intently at the face of his closest collaborator but failed to detect any signs of genuine rebellion. 'Do you want to give up the whole deal?'

'Who's talking about quitting, Perry? But we've been sitting here for weeks, waiting for this confounded monster of a positronic brain to honor us with some information – maybe. All we've heard from it so far is excuses. *The code of this message is extremely difficult to break.* Most likely it will never be deciphered. Who knows – the so-called immortals may have played a dirty trick at our expense.'

Meanwhile another man had joined them. He entered almost unnoticed. He looked like a human being but a certain something in his appearance exuded the impression of superhuman qualities. The tall figure, the uncertain age, the thick, whitish hair, the very high forehead, the reddish albino eyes – and especially the expression in his eyes – all these combined to make him appear ... different. He was a scientist from a star system thirty-four thousand light-years from Earth. The Arkonides, his race, had mastered all the secrets of space travel for thousands of years. Several years ago his research vessel had crash-landed on Earth's moon, where it had been discovered by Perry Rhodan, who rescued the two survivors of the catastrophe, Khrest, the scientist, and the beautiful Thora, the female commander of the research cruiser.

Upon entering Khrest had overheard Bell's last remark. He addressed Bell with a trace of reproach in his voice: 'Aren't you a bit quick to draw such conclusions? The immortals, whose trail we are pursuing, never intended to make our task an easy one.'

'I never doubted that,' replied Bell impatiently. 'Your infallible race found out several thousand years ago that this system contains a planet that is the home of the immortals. But this planet disappeared in the meantime. In order to track it down, we are forced to solve almost impossible tasks, for the inhabitants of the vanished planet have puzzled out a kind of cosmic treasure hunt. Only beings capable of five-dimensional thought processes will be able to find this planet of eternal life. They concocted a real dilly for us poor mortals. We are trying to rack our brains to solve this galactic riddle. And all because we want to find the secret of immortality.'

Perry Rhodan smiled a friendly greeting to Khrest. 'Reg is feeling blue that the positronic brain has not yet deciphered what the coded message of the immortals has to tell us.'

'I'm not feeling blue, I'm sick and tired of waiting around for weeks on end.' Reg sounded disgusted.

The smile had left Rhodan's face. He was serious now as he regarded the giant console of the positronic brain which was hidden behind the huge panels of Arkonite. He knew what must be going on now behind these walls: incomprehensible mechanisms and positronics of superior intelligence were busy translating the encoded message composed in an alien language. Nobody had expected that this message would be easy to decode, particularly in view of the difficulties they had had to overcome to extract it from the underground vault located in the ruling Thort's palace. There the secrets of the vanished race had lain for millennia, hidden in a crypt formed by cosmic rays, which had been made inaccessible by a time lock. The Ferrons had been unable to open the crypt – but Perry Rhodan had succeeded where they had failed.

Now Rhodan's impetuous friend Reginald Bell demanded that these complicated encoded messages be solved instantaneously.

'Whoever seeks eternity must arm himself with infinite patience, Reg,' Rhodan warned. 'We have nothing more urgent to do right now. Everything is fine back home on Earth – otherwise Colonel Freyt would have informed us via hyperwave radio.' Rhodan knew Freyt would use this way of communicating with them only as a last resort. They couldn't risk giving away Earth's position in the universe. There were too many hostile alien races just waiting for such a blunder on their part. Rhodan continued: 'Do you have a better suggestion than continuing to wait for the translated text?'

That was a direct question that deserved a concrete answer. But Bell had no better solution. So he said with an embarrassed grin: 'Unfortunately not, Perry. So I guess we'd better keep on waiting.'

Khrest slowly shook his head with a puzzled expression. 'How strange you humans sometimes behave. There you are discussing things you have agreed upon a long time ago – just because you have too much time on your hands. I would have expected you to come up with a good counterproposal, Reg, if you are dissatisfied with the present state of affairs.'

'I can easily imagine what you have in mind there, Khrest: return to Arkon, to your home planet. I wonder if Thora has been making life miserable for you again with her demands.'

Thora was the former female commander of the shipwrecked Arkonide research vessel on the moon. Ever since she and Khrest had been rescued by Perry Rhodan her overexaggerated self-image had suffered a painful blow. For as far as she was concerned, mankind was at best just at the threshold of truly intelligent life. And this haughty woman had now become dependent on these lowly creatures.

'Why, naturally, it's Thora's desire to return to Arkon; but she sticks to our agreement. First we'll find the planet of eternal life and then we will return to Arkon. Sorry, Bell, but I can't share your views. Rhodan is right, we must first decipher the message of the immortals. Not until then will we know what we must do in order to unravel the mystery of eternal life. It's a goal worth striving for, don't you agree?'

But before Bell could reply, a tiny lamp lit up at the side of a visiscreen. At the same time the dull surface began to glow.

Rhodan flipped a switch. The face of a young man appeared on the screen. His fair hair contrasted sharply with his deeply tanned skin. His lips were pressed together in such a way that he seemed perpetually to grin. But those who were familiar with Major Conrad Deringhouse knew that he rarely smiled indeed. It just looked that way.

'Reporting to the commander!' said Deringhouse. 'The last scouting party of space-fighters has returned from their reconnaissance flight. Nothing special to report from the Vega sector. Shall we keep up our surveillance activities the same as usual?'

'Yes, Deringhouse,' Rhodan acknowledged with a friendly smile, 'keep up the good work! You and Nyssen and the rest of your scouting group mustn't get rusty. Just keep your eyes open.' Rhodan marveled at the enormous job it was to know at all times what was going on, on all the forty-two planets of the system. It was so easy for alien space travelers to land here unnoticed. And unfortunately, as he'd learned by now, those invaders didn't always come with kind intentions. So he added, 'Don't relax your surveillance, Deringhouse!'

'Okay, boss!' Deringhouse confirmed. Then the screen grew dark again. A few minutes later, the small fighter planes would take off to carry out their patrols at the speed of light. Back on Ferrol everybody could rest assured that no one would enter or leave the Vega system unnoticed.

Rhodan turned to Bell. 'You see, everything is quiet here, no immediate danger threatening. Nothing prevents us from waiting in peace and quiet until we get the next clue we need to come nearer to the solution of the galactic riddle that the immortals hatched out more than ten thousand years ago. You must get used to the idea that time plays no role for those who live forever.'

Perry Rhodan could not anticipate how soon this statement would prove to be true. He could not sense yet that time would be the most dangerous factor in the near future. How lucky Rhodan and Bell were to be unaware of that.

The even, monotonous hum of the positronic brain underwent a slight change that did not escape Rhodan's trained ear. He quickly waved off Bell, who was just about to reply. Khrest was listening intently, too. Somewhere behind the massive walls, contacts and relays began to click. Small lamps lit up on the console. Crackling noises came from the loudspeaker system.

For the first time in many weeks, the positronic brain was getting ready to make some statement. Would they now finally learn the meaning of the encoded message left thousands of years ago by those unknowns whose trail they pursued? A message destined only for those intelligent enough to solve the galactic riddle? Would it bring an answer to the question of where the planet of eternal life could be found?

Rhodan's hand trembled imperceptibly as he depressed the small lever underneath the red lamp. The light went out and clicking sounds started in the loud-speaker. Then a metallic voice announced:

'Partial decoding of the message completed. Only the first part could be deciphered. Transcribed written text ready. Use the proper channels to obtain it. Continuing with work for final decoding.'

'A partial solution!' Bell groaned. 'That won't get us very far.'

'Oh, shut up, Reg!' Rhodan was trying hard to overcome his own disappointment. 'You should appreciate that we're finally getting to hear something at least.'

Rhodan's hand moved across the controls of the positronic brain, pushing in several buttons. Little lamps began to glimmer, others grew dark. Somewhere a ticking commenced. A wide slot opened. The three men stared fascinated at this slot, from which they expected the written text to emerge.

But it took almost two minutes until a strip of paper dropped from the opening onto a small table in front of the console, where Rhodan was standing. The type was large and clear. All read the text eagerly:

ONCE THE PLANET ON WHICH YOU ARE NOW STAYING HAS ROTATED 21.3562 TIMES AROUND ITS POLAR AXIS, THE INSCRIPTION WILL FADE AWAY. THERE-FORE HURRY IF YOU WISH TO FIND THE LIGHT.

That was all.

Rhodan tried again to hide his disappointment and worry; he had expected more. But it was one step forward, at least. What was the meaning of this message?

Ferrol rotated around its axis once every 28.23 hours. Shiptime on board the *Stardust* was still reckoned according to the 24 hour day on Terra. Therefore 21.3562 Ferronian days equaled 24.700423 Earth days.

'We found the message exactly three weeks ago in the vault below the Red Palace in Thorta, Ferrol's capital,' Rhodan elaborated. 'That means we have exactly three days and 15 hours left. Or to be precise, the robot brain has that much time left to decipher the rest of the message – or else it will disappear.'

Strange, Bell had been the pessimist just a little while ago. And now, from one moment to the next, he turned optimist. His face was radiant with triumph. 'Well, so what! I don't care if that cosmic inscription vanishes. We have captured it on film! Even if the original should disappear, we still have copies of it.'

Rhodan looked at Khrest. For a moment it seemed that Bell's arguments had made all doubts fade away. Khrest finally reacted to Rhodan's questioning glance.

'My dear Bell, your mistake lies in thinking in a three-dimensional manner. But that does not work if you try to solve the puzzles of those whose minds function on a five-dimensional plane. If they say that this inscription will disappear at a given moment, this includes of course not only the original message but also any copies made of it on film or otherwise.'

Bell's face expressed disbelief. 'But, Khrest, that's quite impossible. How can these immortals exert any influence on our photos? The two are separated from each other by a mere distance of thousands of years! How can you prove your allegation scientifically?'

'That's simple, Bell,' Rhodan intervened. 'I understand what Khrest meant to say when he blamed you for thinking in three-dimensional terms. These immortals think in a five-dimensional way. Time enters their view of the world and mathematical thought in a two-fold manner: first in a form that will perish forever once it has passed; that is the fourth dimension. Then, on a changeable form – let's call it the fifth dimension. All processes of the galactic riddle take place in an automatic fashion. And such an automatic limit is already built-in in this inscription. Once the time limit has passed, an event in the past will be annulled. Therefore, the inscription of the message that our positronic brain is supposed to decode will be totally canceled out. And since the message never was written, it can't exist either in present time – that means, we could never copy it. It simply never existed at any moment in time. You get it?'

Bell's hair stood on end, a sure indication how excited he was. His face mirrored the fight going on inside him; common sense was battling against something incomprehensible.

'But that is—' he started to say.

Rhodan completed his thought: '—something monstrous, I admit. But it is logical, nevertheless. You can bet your life that the writing will disappear in three days and fifteen hours – nothing will ever bring it back again.'

'That's right,' confirmed Khrest.

Bell grew calmer. His inborn intelligence plus the

Arkonide hypno-training that had passed on to him the entire body of knowledge this ancient superior race possessed – these two factors combined made him realize that there was nothing impossible in the universe. There was an explanation for everything, including therefore this seeming contradiction.

'Well,' he decided, 'that leaves us very little time. Let's hope the big brain on the *Stardust* will make it.'

The *Stardust* was the giant spacesphere that once had been seized by a hostile warrior race from the Arkonides. Rhodan had recaptured the ship and thus assured his claim to become the commander of the gigantic battle cruiser. This ship, eight hundred yards in diameter, was the product of a civilization that made Earth appear in contrast like a world inhabited by Stone Age men. The propulsion drive of the *Stardust* permitted space jumps across distances of thousands of light-years with practically no loss of actual time. The ship disposed of audio-visual installations that made possible instantaneous communication within a considerable part of the galaxy. The radio and light waves raced directly through paraspace, rendering any distance totally immaterial.

The *Stardust* was the acme of perfection dreamed of by any human being. The positronic robot brain was only a part of the ship.

'Let's hope that the brain will solve the problem for us,' said Rhodan. 'Otherwise our chase will come to an end and we can redeem our pledge. We will return Thora and Khrest to Arkon.'

'I'm rather scared of that,' declared Bell categorically.

'Frightened? Of what?' Khrest wondered.

'The *Stardust* has filled us with plenty of inferiority complexes. What will happen when we come face to face with the marvels of Arkon, the pivot of the Arkonide galactic empire? Let's be honest with each other, what is Earth compared to Arkon?'

Khrest replied with deadly seriousness, 'A grain of sand – you are quite right.'

There was a definite undertone of pity in his voice.

Was it pity for Bell – or for Earth?

No one could have been able to tell for sure.

Three days went by. The positronic robot had not shown any further success in deciphering the message. Not even partial results had been produced. The gigantic, seemingly all-knowing brain remained silent.

On Ferrol, the eighth planet in the Vega system, everything else went according to plan. Deringhouse was in charge of the patrol flights of his fighter planes. He sent daily reports of their findings to Perry Rhodan. Except for Rhodan's forces and the native Ferrons, there was no sign of any intelligent life in this system. There was nothing to indicate that alien outsiders from other systems had become aware of their existence. The spacefighters carried out their routine patrols among empty and uninhabited worlds.

Meanwhile the Ferronian industry was working at full speed in order to produce exchange goods intended for Earth. Rhodan planned to take them along on his next flight to Terra and exchange them for Terrestrial products. Good trade relations had always been the prerequisite for friendly relations among the various races and nations. How much more important would such relationships become between the races of two worlds that existed twenty-seven light-years apart.

Still, Rhodan was secretly worried about Earth. The Ferrons had a uniform government. They were ruled by one man, the Thort. Earth, on the other hand—

Rhodan sighed. It was true that fear of the technological superiority of the Arkonides, and consequently fear of Rhodan's own power, had united all the governments of the world and thus prevented the outbreak of an atomic war. But this union was only partial. It had not yet brought about one-world government. Below the peaceful surface hatred, distrust and national jealousy were still smoldering.

Perhaps the desired development toward the United States of the world would be speeded up when mankind could see the example of such a political arrangement on Ferrol. And if necessary, thought Rhodan grimly, some prodding from him might help. In any case, Earth must be strong and united, against the day when the Arkonides would discover its position. This he must prevent at all costs, for there was the acute danger that the decadent Arkonides would regard Earth and its inhabitants as a new colony of their star realm.

Rhodan smiled. He knew that things would turn out just the opposite way: Mankind was destined to fall heir to the Arkonide Galactic Empire!

He was sitting all alone in the control center where the positronic brain was housed.

Another thirteen hours, then the time would be up. This could stretch out into an eternity, if you were just sitting and had to wait patiently for the final result from the robot brain. On the other hand, considering that already twenty-four days had gone by without bringing to a successful conclusion the final deciphering of the all-decisive message – then thirteen hours seemed a ridiculously short period.

Rhodan listened to the never-ending hum behind the mighty Arkonide walls. The brain was working at maximum speed, unceasing in its efforts to figure out the text that had been composed ten thousand years ago.

Reginald Bell visited briefly toward noon, making some quite unnecessary remarks. He quickly departed. Khrest and Thora put in a brief appearance, urging Rhodan to inform them immediately about any results coming from the positronic brain. Rhodan was glad to make that promise.

Another eight hours to go!

It was late in the afternoon. Rhodan had quickly eaten a bite but could not be persuaded to interrupt his vigil. Two members of the mutant corps kept him company, the African teleporter Ras Tschubai, and Ralf Marten, the son of a German father and a Japanese mother. Both men belonged to the generation that was born after the first atom bomb explosions on Earth. The parents' genes had been altered as a result of atomic radiation. In many cases this had a positive effect on their descendants: dormant brain functions came to life in these children. They possessed talents that seemed like magic to other men.

Ralf Marten was the so-called teleoptician of the corps. He was capable of separating his mind from his body, letting his mind take over the sense organs of other creatures. He could see with their eyes, hear with

20

their ears and even speak with their mouths. During all this time his own body remained in a cataleptic state, from which he did not recover until he let his own mind return into his own body.

Ras Tschubai was capable of transporting himself over great distances by sheer willpower. His body would dematerialize and then rematerialize at any place he wanted to. He was an excellent teleporter.

The corps comprised many other mutants: telepaths, telekineticists, listeners, direction finders, scouts and frequency-seers. The mutant corps was Rhodan's most reliable troop and most valuable help whenever the necessity arose to represent mankind in an encounter with those extraterrestrial races that possessed super-human qualities.

Ralf Marten and Ras Tschubai tried to help Rhodan while away the time during this most trying period. 'In case the robot brain should fail,' said the African, with a disdainful wave of his large hand, 'not all will be lost. There are other tracks we can follow up. Just remember the pyramid on the outer moon of the thirteenth planet. The Ferronian scientist Lossoshér discovered it. You said yourself that the inscription found on this pyramid represented a further step, even if it was only a detour that eventually would lead you nearer to your goal. Okay, so let's take this detour, if the direct route proves to be too difficult.'

'The direct route is the fastest way, Ras – we can't afford to waste any time. The Arkonides are getting impatient. They want to return to their home planet. We've been putting them off for years now. Only their desire to find the planet of eternal life – a wish we share with them – has so far kept them from insisting more rigorously on their very justified demands.'

'We shouldn't give up hope yet,' said Ralf Marten. 'Let's hope the brain will come through in time, even if twenty-four days have passed without much result.'

'That's what's bothering me,' admitted Rhodan. 'If twenty-four days were not enough time to find the solution, what can it still accomplish in barely eight hours? It doesn't look too good, I'm afraid.'

Ras Tschubai was just about to say something when he suddenly changed his mind. He listened. The hum behind the walls sounded different now. It grew stronger and more irregular. Several control lamps lit up. Whole rows of lamps flashed in regular intervals, as if they were trying to give some signal.

It was a signal indeed. A sharp click came from the loudspeaker. Then followed the expressionless voice of the robot brain, revealing neither passion nor triumph:

FINISHED DECODING THE MESSAGE. TEXT WILL BE GIVEN IN WRITING.

Rhodan lost not a second to inform Khrest and Thora as promised. He also called Bell over the intercom to come to the control center.

While the three were on their way, and hurriedly entering the room, the slip with the text was expelled from a narrow slot in the console. The typed text could be clearly read the very instant the paper emerged from the positronic brain.

IF YOU KNOW SOMETHING ABOUT OUR
LIGHT, YOU MUST SEEK OUT THE ONE
FROM WHOM YOU OBTAINED THIS
KNOWLEDGE. ONLY ONE PERSON WAS
AMAZED BY THE MACHINES OF KNOWL-
EDGE – THIS WAS IN RECENT TIMES, JUST
A FEW SECONDS AGO ACCORDING TO MY
CHRONOLOGY. SEEK HIM OUT AND ASK
HIM! IF YOU WANT TO FIND HIM, THEN
YOU MUST COME TO THE CRYPT OF THE
LIGHT, BUT DO NOT COME WITHOUT
SOME INFORMATION ABOUT HIS PERSON.
YOU WILL BE ASKED WHAT HIS NAME IS.

Rhodan took the piece of paper and stared at the
clearly printed letters that formed comprehensible words
– yet their meaning was vague and mysterious. He read
the text three times before he passed it on to Khrest,
who in turn read it swiftly. Something akin to disappointment swept across his features as he gave Thora
the printed message. She apparently could not make any
sense out of the report either. Bell did not really give her
much chance to do so; he did not even take the trouble
to ask her permission. He simply grabbed the paper
from her hands and devoured the few lines as if his life
depended on it. His disillusionment was all the greater.
He looked rather puzzled as he returned the paper to
Rhodan.

'I can't figure it out. Who is this person that you're
supposed to find, Perry?'

'Right now I'm at a loss, the same as you. But I'm
confident that we'll soon know what the immortals have

in mind with these words. Let's try to examine them from a logical point of view. The positronic brain could probably be of help here. But with some effort we can arrive at the meaning by ourselves. We're supposed to find someone who recently expressed amazement at the machines of great knowledge. Question: what are these machines? And: what do the immortals understand by "in recent times, just a few seconds ago according to my chronology"? First we'll have to clear up these two questions, if we count on learning whose name they wish to hear from us.'

'The machines of knowledge,' remarked Khrest softly, 'could very well be the matter transmitters which are in the Ferrons' possession.'

Rhodan realized immediately that Khrest had found the answer to the first part of the question. The matter transmitters had been given to the Ferrons some ten thousand years ago by an unknown space-traveling race. At that time the Ferrons were still a rather primitive people who had done some favor for the strangers whose spaceship had become stranded on the planet Ferrol. As a token of gratitude the strangers had presented them with one of the marvels of their superior technology. These matter transmitters were still in excellent working order, although the Ferrons could not understand how they functioned. Their construction was based on five-dimensional mathematics; they transported matter through hyperspace.

Who had expressed astonishment about these instruments? Or better: *Who* had been amazed by them and *when* had this taken place?

'We must proceed logically and draw our conclusions,' Rhodan said. 'There is one clue here: I must seek out the person who first told me about the light. The light, of course, represents immortality. You Khrest, originally spoke of this to me. Your expedition had started out several years ago to find the planet of eternal life. Therefore you're the first key person to this puzzle. Now all we need do is to ascertain your source of information.'

'That's quite simple, Perry,' replied Khrest. 'I learned about this from the central master file back on Arkon. Our scientific council entrusted us with the mission to locate the planet of immortality. Therefore, some records must exist about this planet. They should go back to that era in our history when our ancestors were busy exploring the universe. That is probably when they encountered the race of immortals, but our index files contain the names of many thousands of expeditions. How can we be sure to pick the right one?'

'This shouldn't present too many difficulties, Khrest. We should concentrate our efforts on those Arkonides that explored the immediate vicinity of Earth some ten thousand years ago. They most likely met up somewhere along the way with the immortals – or found their trace. That particular expedition, or maybe several groups, must be the same that built your base on the planet Venus, where they constructed the mightiest of all existing positronic brains. We know that these Arkonides then settled on Earth, where they merged and became part of the bloodstream of humanity. Who knows what catastrophes helped along this process – perhaps Atlantis. We can assume with certainty that some report must have reached your home planet –

otherwise no such records would have been registered in your central file. And you, Khrest, and Thora, would never have been sent to Earth.'

Thora nodded her head eagerly. 'Of course, you're quite right! Now we must find the name of that commander who sent this report about his research expedition. We have no choice now, we must fly at once to Arkon and look for this information in our central registry.'

Thora's voice was triumphant. Bell looked at the beautiful Arkonide woman with alarm. He could not make up his mind whether he liked or hated her. He was suspicious of her motives. Yes, she was beautiful indeed. Her white hair contrasted very effectively with her lovely tanned skin. Her reddish albino eyes revealed wisdom but also arrogance. Was she driven by the same emotions as Terrestrials? Bell doubted it – but he might be quite mistaken.

Rhodan smiled. 'You're wrong, Thora. I'm sorry to have to tell you this. We don't need to fly to Arkon in order to find out the name of that man who sent this particular report to the central file on Arkon those many years ago. That expedition must no doubt also have been here in the Vega system. But if they did not return home, and still informed Arkon about their encounter with the immortals, then this news must have been sent from the base on Venus. And everything that happened there has been registered by the positronic brain. You see, Thora, the solution to our problem is quite simple: we fly to Venus and ask the positronic brain there.'

Thora had to agree, even though it did not make her too happy. 'Yes, very simple, Perry. And what will be the next step once you learn that name?'

Rhodan pointed to the slip of paper that was lying on the little table in front of the console. 'The message here tells me what to do. I'll memorize the name and then descend once more into the underground vault of the light on Thorta. The rest will follow all by itself.'

Bell could no longer restrain himself. He had kept his mouth shut while Rhodan was arguing with Khrest and Thora. But now he burst out full of excitement. 'We'll fly back to home sweet home then before we have to go down again into the crypt under the Red Palace on Thorta. Does that mean we'll have to return also to that horrible machine hall that nearly finished us off last time we followed the trail of the immortals?'

'I would rather doubt that, Reggie. We'll just descend into the underground vault ... then we'll wait and see. I think this time the unknown race might have some other riddle in store for us to solve. Who knows?'

Little did he know how right he was in his assumption.

2. THE STORY OF KERLON

They were ready for takeoff. Destination: Earth. Rhodan had decided to leave behind on Ferrol a squadron of space-fighter planes under the command of Major Rod Nyssen, together with fifty-four pilots. This move offered a twofold advantage. The first extraterrestrial combined trading post and military base of the New Power – as the alliance between Arkonides and Perry Rhodan's group was known – was thus adequately protected. Besides, space was vacated in the giant hangars aboard the *Stardust*, which could now be used to store huge quantities of Ferronian goods. These unique and technologically superior products, so far unknown on Earth, would be in great demand. Rhodan was certain to make a tremendous profit on the first merchandise to be imported to Terra from a far distant solar system. And money was always needed for further development and expansion of the New power.

The *Stardust* first went into orbit around Ferrol, the eighth planet of the Vega system, and then took off into the vastness of space. The Arkonide spaceship cut across the various orbital paths of the Vegan planets. It traveled at simple speed of light. Only several hours later it reached the depth of interstellar space, where the transition could take place. Otherwise the ensuing shock to the space-time structure might have endangered the orbits of the Vegan planets around their sun.

The coordinates were set.

As usual, the crew was seized by a familiar sensation of excitement that preceded the transition. There was no actual danger but a jump through hyperspace was still an awe-inspiring event for the sober mind. Ship and crew would simply cease to exist – at least in the third dimension. Time affected the event in two ways: while accelerating and retarding, they would be transported through a distance of twenty-seven light-years within just a few hours and without noticing anything.

The hyperjump, however, would cause a wrench in the structure of the entire universe, which would be transmitted simultaneously everywhere without any loss of time. Certain intelligent races existed somewhere in the depths of space. They had constructed instruments capable of registering and locating the origin of the warp rupture. These warp-sensors constituted a threat for those who wished to remain undetected. For the time being Rhodan preferred that no one would learn of mankind's existence.

Therefore each hyperjump represented a risk.

Everything went off smoothly, as far as they could determine. They had no way of knowing, of course, whether this warp rupture had been registered by some-one somewhere out in space, perhaps a hundred or even ten thousand light-years away. All Rhodan could do now was hope for the best.

The *Stardust* materialized again far outside the crew's native solar system. Sol appeared as a very bright yellow-white star straight ahead in direct line of flight.

Rhodan sat up on his contour couch in order to see the sun on the visiscreen in the Command Center.

Bell entered. He had preferred to stay in his own cabin during the transition. 'Is that Sol?' he inquired, pointing to the image on the visiscreen.

Rhodan simply nodded without speaking. He was busy typing navigational inquiries into the computer's keyboard. The answers came almost instantaneously on perforated strips of paper that flowed forth in a steady stream from the output slot. Rhodan inserted the beginning of this paper strip in the input of another computer, which in turn evaluated the results. The *Stardust* automatically was set on the correct course.

Venus was on the other side of the sun.

Three hours later they passed Pluto. They established contact via radio with the observation base on Pluto, which was on constant lookout for the appearance of unidentified alien spaceships in order to report such occurrences at once to the center in Galacto-City on Terra. In case of such an event Colonel Freyt had been instructed to inform Rhodan by way of hyperwave radio.

In another ten hours Venus was visible as a bright crescent that grew constantly larger. Sol's second planet had turned out to be inhabitable for human beings. It was home to antediluvian giant reptiles and a species of semi-intelligent seals who lived in the numerous oceans. The climate was tropical and humid. The oxygen content of the air in the lowlands was sufficient for human beings, while the lighter hydrogen made the upper strata of the Venusian atmosphere unfit for man. A heavy cloud cover shrouded the planet's surface. There was frequent and heavy rain.

The atmosphere's carbon dioxide content presented an additional difficulty. It was higher than on Earth but not in critical concentrations. One Venusian day lasted two hundred forty Earth hours. The gravity near the planet's equator was less than on Earth, just 0.85 G's.

Ten thousand years ago the Arkonides had established a giant base on Venus. They had hollowed out a huge mountain and then built their base inside. The Arkonides had long since vanished from their Venusian stronghold but their technical installations and robots had remained and now obeyed the commands of Rhodan and his friends.

In case a non-Arkonide spaceship would approach the fortified mountain base, mighty defensive weapons were programmed to ward off the intruders. Nothing but the gigantic fleet of a highly intelligent race, that had been schooled in millennia of constant warfare, would have even a chance to overcome the mechanical defense system of ancient Arkonides.

One of the entrances to the underground labyrinth was located on the high plateau of the mountain. The *Stardust* was slowly approaching this relatively flat area. Invisible probing rays examined the ship and permitted it to come in for a landing.

Inside the mountain fortress was the giant positronic brain. It knew already that one of the ships of its ancient builders was coming near.

Only Rhodan and Khrest had set foot on Venus. They intended to obtain information from the omniscient robot brain. Meanwhile Reginald Bell was in charge of the *Stardust*. Rhodan had issued orders that the giant spacesphere was to return to Galacto-City, the New Power's main base on Earth.

Galacto-City! The most modern metropolis of the world, built in the middle of the Gobi Desert on the Asian continent. Its site was on the very spot where a few years earlier Rhodan had landed upon his return from the first trip to the moon, accompanied by Khrest and Thora, the two shipwrecked Arkonides whom he had rescued. Near the shores of the Goshun salt lake he had erected his first base, defying the violent protests of all the governments of the world. Now the base had grown tremendously. Robots and automated robot machines had constructed this vast city surrounding the actual center whose valuable installations were protected by a permanent energy dome. The entire area of the New Power's realm covered some twenty-four thousand square miles, protected from the outside world by Rhodan's army.

These armed forces consisted of five hundred superbly trained soldiers equipped with Arkonide weapons. They were ably assisted by some five thousand Arkonide robot soldiers, programmed to obey only Rhodan's orders or those of his authorized personel.

Four battleships, huge spacespheres of Arkonide design, swift space-fighters, all heavily armed, made up the city's defense forces that served only one purpose: to maintain peace!

The commander in charge of these forces during

Rhodan's absence was Colonel Freyt, who so closely resembled Rhodan that he could have been mistaken for his brother.

Colonel Freyt was standing in Galacto-City's spaceport, awaiting the announced arrival of the *Stardust*. As soon as the gigantic ship had safely settled on the ground he started walking over to the passenger exit. He gazed up at the spaceship that now looked like an incredibly tall building. The convex hull of shiny metal arched upward reaching into the blue sky. He came closer and the metal wall was hanging almost horizontally above him. The exit hatch opened and Reginald Bell's stocky figure appeared. He quickly slid down the moving belt, almost tumbling into the arms of his waiting friend.

'Welcome home, Reggie!' Freyt saluted a bit sloppily. 'Or to make it quite official: On behalf of the New Power we welcome our Minister of Defense. . . . Everything is okay here at the base.'

'That's what I like to hear,' roared Bell, slapping Freyt's back in a friendly greeting. 'Rhodan and Khrest have remained on Venus. Thora has returned with us. Here she comes.'

Freyt was surely not the only man who took pleasure in looking at the beautiful Arkonide woman, even if she comported herself in a cool, distant and haughty manner. Still, she was a woman, and an extraordinarily gorgeous female at that.

'Why are you staring at me, Colonel Freyt?' Thora inquired. 'Have I changed so much?'

'You just looked tanned, very becoming,' Freyt stammered, embarrassed. He was furious at the same time because of Bell's impertinent grin. 'You feel fine, I hope.'

'Thank you. I always feel great when I have a chance to get rid of that pest Bell for a few days.' Thora spoke in a condescending way. I'm looking forward to not having to see this Earthling as long as we're here in Galacto-City.'

Bell kept on grinning broadly. He turned to Freyt. 'She's true to form. Have fun! She'll probably ask you to be at her beck and call. Show her a good time in the city while I'm busy supervising the unloading and loading of exchange goods for our Ferronian allies.'

'Great! Everything is ready for you,' Freyt replied gratefully. 'As far as I'm concerned you can start right away with that job.'

'That can wait till tomorrow, my friend. Where's the nearest bar?'

In the meantime some of the mutants had disembarked, as well as Dr. Haggard and Dr. Manoli, the two physicians. Freyt welcomed everyone, carrying on brief conversations with the returning crew, until the first transport gliders arrived. The unloading of the ship's freight began immediately.

Freyt took Bell by the arm and pulled him aside. 'I have some good news for Rhodan,' he said mysteriously. 'It won't be long now until we'll have one united government of the world. Our negotiations have progressed splendidly. Mankind still hasn't forgotten the narrow escape we had some time ago from alien invaders. And to think that mankind was in danger of exterminating itself! We were on the brink of an atomic war! Only their fear of the boomerang effect of a total

34

atomic war, of falling victim to a general holocaust, prevented them from jumping right into it. But now they seem to be willing to listen to the voice of reason.'

'That's great news,' commented Bell. He was bursting with all the tall tales he loved to tell whenever he returned from one of their space trips. 'I haven't done so bad myself, Freyt. I've solved part of the galactic riddle.'

Freyt's face changed into a question mark. 'What riddle did you say?'

Bell grinned. 'That's a long story that's best told over a few drinks. Now take me to the nearest bar, pal. You know Rhodan believes alcohol is only fit to be used for medicinal purposes. And I haven't been sick for a long time!'

The metallic conveyor belts rolled eerily through the underground corridors of the rocky fortress. The walls were illuminated by a faint glow. The hum of mighty generators could be heard coming from somewhere. From time to time Khrest and Rhodan were sliding by the openings of some smaller side corridors that led deeper into the mountain base. Silently and clumsily, robots moved alongside the conveyor belt. They did not react when Khrest and Rhodan passed by. Their probing rays received the brainwave patterns of the two men, checked and registered them. These apparently harmless looking machine creatures would have quickly changed into death-dealing monsters if these brainwave patterns had not been of the correct type.

One day had passed – one Earthday.

'I wonder whether we will get an answer today,' ventured Khrest.

'Maybe,' Rhodan replied. 'We've done all we could. We've presented our questions and all the necessary particulars to the positronic brain. Twenty-four hours are a long time. We should get a partial answer, at least.'

Once again they passed by a side corridor. They knew where it led: to the completely automated command Center of the defense installations. From this point the entire planet Venus could be defended against whole fleets of attacking hostile ships. And perhaps even the entire solar system might be protected this way.

Now the conveyor belt slowed down. They were approaching their destination, the center that housed the brain. This positronic brain was similar to that on board the *Stardust*. It had the same controls, yet it was much bigger, all encompassing, omniscient.

Its memories reached back for thousands of years.

In addition to that this brain on Venus had another inestimable advantage. It could conjure up thought images upon a screen. The observer could visually follow the descriptions of events the brain was thinking about.

If desired, one could thus see an actual filmic report of happenings thousands of years earlier. Perhaps even, Rhodan thought, a bit frightened, a report coming from the future.

All these thoughts passed through Rhodan's mind while the conveyor belt came to a standstill. They had arrived.

The corridor ended in front of a big metal door. Khrest and Rhodan stepped up to it, stopping about one yard short of the door. They knew that they were being observed and examined at this point by invisible and mechanical eyes. Then the door slid noiselessly open.

The entrance to the Command Center of the positronic brain lay wide open in front of them.

The light came on; everything was now brightly lit up ahead. The giant console came to life. Little lamps began to glow, then grew dark again. Levers began to move. The hum from behind the walls grew stronger. The positronic brain obviously must have been expecting them, for hardly had they sat down at their listening posts than the loudspeaker spoke up with its impersonal mechanical voice:

THE INFORMATION YOU SUPPLIED HAS BEEN CHECKED. THE MEMORY BANKS HAVE GIVEN THE DESIRED ANSWERS. THE RESULT WILL BE TRANSMITTED TO YOU IN THE FORM OF A FILM. AT THE SAME TIME YOU WILL RECEIVE A SHORTENED VERSION IN THE FORM OF A WRITTEN REPORT. IF YOU WISH TO HAVE A TAPE RECORD OF THIS REPORT, PLEASE PUSH THE RECORDING BUTTON. THE REPORT WILL START IN ONE MINUTE.

The loudspeaker fell silent.
Khrest looked at Rhodan. 'What do you think?'
'Let's just watch the film, Khrest. All we really need

is the name of the man who once upon a time landed on Ferrol and expressed astonishment at the sight of the matter transmitters. There's no record of this event in the Ferronian annals. They've never mentioned to us that somebody else landed on their planet after the immortal race had been there. Secondly, we'll need to know the approximate date of this event. These two items will be covered in the short written version of the report... The film is about to begin.'

A wall panel had rolled aside and a picture screen appeared. The dull glass began to glow softly, giving way shortly to an abstract color design. This lasted just a few seconds, then a true to life three-D film started to roll. It was an authentic film, even if it portrayed events that had taken place thousands of years ago. Three giant spacespheres hovered in infinite space. They approached a solar system at the speed of light. They cruised about for a while and finally landed on the system's sole inhabited planet. There they were greeted with awe and reverence by the shy native population.

The tinny, mechanical voice of the positronic brain carried on a running commentary, while the film was showing.

9,985 TERRESTRIAL YEARS AGO COMMANDER KERLON AND HIS FLEET OF THREE EXPLORATORY SPACE CRUISERS REACHED THE VEGA SYSTEM, WHICH CONSISTED OF FORTY-THREE PLANETS. A BRIEF SCOUTING TOUR REVEALED THAT ONLY THE EIGHTH PLANET WAS INHABITED BY INTELLIGENT LIFE. KERLON

LANDED AND WAS WELCOMED BY THE
NATIVES, WHO SEEMED SOMEWHAT
FRIGHTENED OF THEM. SOON THE AR-
KONIDE ASTRONAUTS LEARNED THAT
THEY HAD NOT BEEN THE FIRST 'GODS'
TO ARRIVE ON FERROL (THE NATIVES'
NAME FOR THEIR HOME PLANET). OTHERS
HAD MADE AN EMERGENCY LANDING
THERE. THE NATIVES WERE FRIENDLY
AND HELPED THEIR 'GUESTS,' WHO IN AP-
PRECIATION FOR THIS ASSISTANCE LEFT
SEVERAL MATTER TRANSMITTERS
BEHIND. THE ARKONIDE EXPLORERS HAD
MERELY SOME THEORETICAL KNOWL-
EDGE OF SUCH DEVICES, BUT HAD SO FAR
BEEN UNABLE TO BUILD THEM.'

Now the film showed how the Ferrons led the Arkonides to the matter transmitters.

KERLON EXPRESSED AMAZEMENT AT
THE SIGHT OF THESE TECHNICAL
MARVELS AND WANTED TO KNOW
FURTHER DETAILS ABOUT THESE MA-
CHINES. THE FERRONS TOLD THAT THEY
HAD RECEIVED THEM AS A GIFT FROM
THOSE BEINGS THAT 'LIVED LONGER
THAN THE SUN.' THIS WAS IN REFERENCE
TO THE RACE OF THE IMMORTALS.
KERLON WAS GREATLY ASTONISHED BUT
HE DID NOT REPORT THIS INCIDENT
UNTIL MUCH LATER TO THE CENTRAL

MASTER FILE ON ARKON. HE SENT THIS REPORT FROM THE SECOND PLANET OF STILL ANOTHER SOLAR SYSTEM.

THE THREE ARKONIDE EXPLORATORY VESSELS STARTED OUT AGAIN AND WENT BEYOND THE VEGA SYSTEM. THEN THEY MADE A TRANSITION JUMP THROUGH HYPERSPACE, COMING OUT AGAIN INTO NORMAL SPACE WITHIN THE OTHER SOLAR SYSTEM. THERE THEY LANDED ON THE SECOND PLANET, CALLED VENUS. KERLON AND HIS MEN CONSTRUCTED A GIANT BASE THERE AND SENT OFF DETAILED REPORTS OF THEIR TRAVELS TO ARKON. THESE REPORTS WERE DULY RECEIVED, REGISTERED AND RECORDED. LATER ON, KERLON'S EXPEDITIONARY FORCES SETTLED TERRA, THE SYSTEM'S THIRD PLANET. KERLON MET HIS DEATH WHILE FIGHTING THE SAVAGES OF A HUGE CONTINENT. THIS ISLAND WORLD WAS LATER ATTACKED BY ENEMIES COMING FROM OUTER SPACE. AS A RESULT THIS CONTINENT PERISHED, SINKING INTO THE OCEAN.

The monotone voice of the robot brain continued:

KERLON HAS LONG SINCE BEEN DEAD. HE WAS THE FIRST ARKONIDE TO RUN ACROSS THE TRAIL OF THE IMMORTAL

RACE – AND TO LOSE TRACK OF THEM AGAIN. KERLON WAS ALSO THE FIRST ARKONIDE TO ENCOUNTER AND WONDER ABOUT THE MATTER TRANSMITTERS AND TO SEND HOME AN ACCOUNT. FURTHER DETAILS, HOWEVER, WERE LOST. THE ARKONIDE POPULATION ON VENUS VANISHED. ALL THAT REMAIN THERE ARE THE ROBOTS AND ALL THE STORED INFORMATION.'

The film was over. The screen grew dark. The voice fell silent.

Rhodan remained seated in front of the quiescent robot brain. The humming sound from behind the walls had ceased. Rhodan was pondering what he had just witnessed. For the first time he realized that an insurmountable wall stood between him and the solution of the galactic riddle. What use was it now to have learned the name of the man who had wondered at the matter transmitters, if that same man had been dead for the past ten thousand years Kerlon and Rhodan were separated by a millennial barrier of time.

There was nothing to be learned from the Ferrons. The film had made that quite clear. They had lived in a primitive feudal society at the time of the first Arkonide landing on Ferrol. The Ferronian weapons consisted of old-fashioned muzzle-loaders, swords and lances. They wore suits of armor like medieval warriors had done on Earth. No memory of this second encounter with alien visitors had survived. The natives had probably been too preoccupied with internecine warfare and strife.

'Now we know this man's name – Kerlon – but that is all. What next, Perry?' Khrest's voice sounded rather discouraged.

Rhodan abruptly stood up. 'We'll see. After all, they didn't ask for anything else, just the name of that man. That's what we were supposed to find out and we did. We'll get our next answer inside the vault in the Thort's palace on Thorta. We'll fly back to Earth now and from there we'll return to Ferrol. We'll discover there whether we've lost the trail to the planet of eternal life or not.'

Khrest also rose. 'The auxiliary vessel is waiting outside the fortress to bring us back to Earth. I'm looking forward to seeing your home planet once again, Perry.'

Rhodan glanced quizzically at the Arkonide scientist but the latter's voice had been totally devoid of sarcasm.

Reginald Bell was in his element.

He had to select two hundred men from among the soldiers and specialist workers of the New Power. From now on they were supposed to serve on the *Stardust*. This would increase the number of the spaceship's crew to five hundred. Added to this number was the Mutant Corps and the inner circle of command.

It was a difficult task to decide which of the many volunteers were most qualified to become members of the *Stardust*'s crew. One of the criteria, Rhodan had decreed, was the volunteers' marital status. They should not have strong family ties. Married people were out therefore.

But this did not apply only to men. Numerous females were chosen for service on the *Stardust*. All had to be single. All that mattered then were their professional qualifications as wireless operators, electronic specialists or chemists. From now on women physicians and technicians would work aboard the spaceship and help to represent the human race on interstellar trips. Bell noticed, not without satisfaction, that the male members of the old crew accepted this new regime with definite signs of approval.

Bell's strenuous task came to a sudden end with Rhodan's return from Venus. Since the unloading of Ferronian and loading of Terrestrial goods had been completed in the meantime, nothing stood in the way of the *Stardust*'s departure.

Three days after Khrest's and Rhodan's arrival on Earth the *Stardust* was ready for takeoff.

The *Stardust* shot up once again into the blue skies that enveloped Earth with a mantle which hid from human eyes the terrifying loneliness and immensity of the universe. The ship flew beyond Pluto, using simple speed of light, soon reaching the point of transition.

The gigantic sphere suddenly started to oscillate as if it were surrounded by an envelope of hot air. Soon everything vanished from sight.

The shockwave, resulting from the warp disturbance of the space-time structure, was propagated with unimaginable speed throughout the universe, reaching its very edges without any loss of time.

But inside the universe lived innumerable races on innumerable planets. And once again Rhodan was fearful that one of these races might possess some instruments resembling the Arkonide warp-sensors and therefore would become aware of the *Stardust*'s hyperjump.

This most certainly would cause them to wonder as to the origin of this transition through hyperspace.

3. BATTLE IN THE PAST

The Thort, ruler of all Ferrons, seemed greatly impressed by the goods Rhodan had brought along from Earth. His trade organizations did splendid business with the Terrestrial merchandise. Thus both he and Rhodan were highly satisfied with the financial success of these transactions. The first interstellar trade relations between the two races had been established.

Rhodan charged Major Deringhouse to supervise the unloading of the goods. Rhodan was restless. He realized this was due to the uncertainty about their real mission: the solving of the galactic riddle. Hardly had Deringhouse left, when Rhodan summoned Bell, Khrest, Thora, Dr Haggard and John Marshall, the telepath. Nothing would prevent him from descending this very day into the crypt underneath the Red Palace.

However there were a few items he wanted to discuss first with his closest collaborators.

'You all remember the decoded message,' Rhodan began, and held up the paper containing the text which barely a week ago the positronic brain had translated for them. 'There are three points in it for us to consider. To begin with, the immortals speak of seconds that have passed. We may safely assume that these seconds have lasted exactly almost ten thousand years. Next: the message ordered us to find the man who had wondered about the machines of knowledge and to ask him. This presents us with a problem: what was meant by that? We did find that man, at least we learned his name. But how can you question someone who has been dead for these past ten thousand years? I'm afraid that this part of the galactic riddle will defy solution. Finally the message tells us to come down into the underground vault in order to interrogate that man. This must be interpreted to mean that there is some possibility to talk to a dead man via the fifth dimension. Don't ask me how this works – I really don't have an explanation for it. Anyhow, we will soon find out. For I'm not descending into the crypt without knowing the name of the man, Kerlon. There is still some point in that message that has aroused my curiosity. . . .'

Rhodan stopped for a moment and looked at his friends. Thora was listening intently and Rhodan thought he detected a trace of admiration in her eyes. Khrest remained quiet, as did Haggard and Marshall. Only Bell was wriggling in his seat as if he could no longer contain his impatient feelings. There was a mute request in his eyes to wind up the whole affair as fast and painlessly as possible.

Rhodan did him that favor.

'The exact wording of the message was: . . . *just a few seconds according to my chronology.* The emphasis here is on the word *my*. The logical conclusion therefore is that there is only *one* immortal being!'

Absolute silence reigned in the cabin for a long time. Khrest looked as if he had been suddenly sentenced to death. Thora's mouth stood slightly open in amazement at this announcement and Bell stared wide-eyed, utterly perplexed.

Haggard and Marshall were the first to break the silence. Both spoke at the same time: 'Only *one* immortal being! That's a paradox! Impossible!'

'Possible!' Rhodan replied coldly. 'It is absolutely within the realm of possibility and I will tell you why. Way back when the immortals landed on Ferrol they were still existing as a race. Then, for unknown reasons, they decided to emigrate from the system. At the same time some catastrophe befell them which brought about the extinction of their race, despite their immortality. Only one of them survived. He did not want to keep the secret for himself and decided to find a worthy successor. He devised the galactic riddle. Whoever could solve it would be rewarded with the secret of eternal life. He set the trail, probably later than we originally assumed. We found his trail and have been pursuing it ever since. As far as I'm concerned, there's nothing paradoxical now in speaking of the "immortal" rather then referring to his whole race that lived longer than the sun. Their sun must have set much too soon for them!'

'Only *one* immortal being,' Khrest murmured pensively. 'Your explanation, Perry, is more than fantastic. It is monstrous!'

'What kind of a creature would that be?' Thora asked softly. 'A creature that poses riddles that demand extraordinary intelligence to solve – and not only that: whose solution requires the knowledge of gigantic brains? A being that has control over time?'

'Yes,' Rhodan agreed. 'It is capable of controlling

time. And this is what renders it immortal. We shall go down to the underground vault and request an answer. I'd like you to accompany me. Today!'

Khrest demurred. 'Without the mutants?'

'We'll take along John Marshall, the telepath. Perhaps also our telekineticist, Anne Sloane.'

'How about our robot?' Bell interjected.

Everyone knew who was meant by that. They had trained one of the Arkonide robots by connecting him directly to the positronic brain. He had thus become capable of five-dimensional thought. The immeasurable memory banks and logisma-gears had turned him into a superintelligent machine creature who had become an indispensable member during their search. No one could predict what emergencies they might encounter.

'All right then,' Rhodan finally gave his consent. 'This time the following people will accompany me: Khrest, Bell, Marshall, Anne Sloane, Dr Haggard and the robot. Thora, wouldn't you like to join us this time?'

Their eyes met. Rhodan recognized that she would prefer to accompany him out of sheer defiance. But then her feminine prudence won out. 'Since Khrest is going along with you, I suppose it will be wiser for me to stay behind. Sort of a precautionary measure, a safety device.'

Bell suggested: 'Why shouldn't a few more of the mutants come with us? At least our teleporter Ras Tschubai. Perhaps also Ralf Marten. He's always complaining that he has to stay too much in the background.'

'Okay with me,' Rhodan agreed shortly. 'Will you please inform the others. Our matter transmitter to the Red Palace will accommodate just nine persons. We'll leave in thirty minutes.'

Ages before, the immortal, whose trail they were trying to track down, had erected a ray-vault beneath the palace of the Ferronian ruler. The vault was invisible to the naked eye. It was formed by beams of rays, consisting of the waves of far distant radio stars. The Arkonide generator was the only machine capable of neutralizing these waves. It caused the crypt to materialize in present time and to take on three-dimensional form.

Rhodan pushed the button to start the generator. Almost instantaneously their environment changed. Where shortly before had been nothing but a vault steeped in semidarkness, a glistening cone had appeared. It seemed to have come from nowhere. Gradually the glowing ray-cone dissolved. Now objects became visible inside the large underground hall. Yet the matter transmitter was not among them.

In the spot where formerly the transmitter had stood was now a chair. It was poised on a low dais. The chair seemed to beckon one to sit down in it. It was the only object that now remained where the cone had been.

Rhodan deliberated briefly, then concluded: He was supposed to sit down in this chair, of course! The rest would follow by itself. The chair would supply the first answer they were seeking.

Khrest, too, had recognized the significance of the chair. 'This chair represents the link to the immortal.

Anyone of us can take a seat in it, Rhodan, for we all are familiar with the name of the man in the past who expressed amazement.'

'I'll do it,' said Rhodan. 'If anyone has to take a risk, I prefer to be the one. Khrest, you wait here with the others. Observe closely whatever will take place. Come to my assistance if necessary.'

Bell obviously wanted to make a comment but held himself back. His lips were pressed tightly together. Fine perspiration beaded his forehead.

'And in case you should vanish from sight . . .?' Ras Tschubai asked.

Rhodan quickly glanced at the African. 'Then you'll follow me. After all, that's what teleporters are here for.'

The African smiled quizzically. 'I can surmount space but not time.'

Rhodan did not reply. He straightened up with determination and walked over to the chair. In the few seconds it took him to reach the chair, all details about it became imprinted on his mind.

The seat was not upholstered, it was just a smooth metal surface. The back consisted of metal, too. It seemed to blink at him maliciously. The plump legs were anchored to the ground. The seat was unusually thick and massive.

Rhodan stood in front of the chair. He hesitated.

What would happen when he sat down in it? The message had warned him and insisted he come here only if he knew the name of the person who had wondered about the transmitter. All right, he did know that name. So he qualified in that respect.

He took one last step and climbed upon the podium. Then he sat down in the chair.

The metal felt warm to the touch, as if someone had been sitting in it a short while ago. That was all he felt. But while Rhodan was still waiting for something to occur, things began to happen lightning fast, taking him by surprise.

A hum started below; the machine began to operate. The entire subterranean hall began to vibrate. An energy screen lit up simultaneously. It enveloped Rhodan and the chair with the podium. Rhodan perceived Khrest, Bell and the others as from behind a thin veil, but all sounds had ceased abruptly. He was all alone under the energy dome, totally cut off from the outside world, although he could still see it. Then even this vanished.

It grew dark around him. Only the energy dome shed a weak fluorescent light, not enough to make things recognizable. Rhodan became aware that some alien force began to invade his mind. He resisted this attempt instinctively but soon abandoned it. It would have been senseless to avoid the questions that were being posed to his subconscious. He did not even know whether he would be able to answer them. His resistance died down fully once he realized that it could only harm him to continue to offer it. With a sense of well-being he felt how the unknown entity suddenly and completely took possession of his mind.

This lasted but a few seconds, then it became light again, while at the same time the energy screen disappeared. The vibration below the metal seat stopped; the hum ceased. Rhodan peered into the eagerly questioning faces of his friends.

'Where have you been?' asked Bell. 'You disappeared from view.'

'So did you.' answered Rhodan, and rose from his seat. He remained standing next to the chair; he could not tell exactly why. What held him back?

It came to him in a flash: the answer! Where was the answer the immortal had promised?

Meanwhile the others crowded around him. Khrest and Bell both inquired excitedly: 'What happened?'

'I couldn't say for sure what was taking place but I assume that something thoroughly examined my memory. The immortal – or his creation – must have found out by now that I know the name of the man who ten thousand years ago was surprised to see matter transmitters that operate on the fifth-dimensional principle on the primitive, semi-barbaric planet Ferrol. That was the condition the immortal had requested us to fulfil. We did our part, now it is up to him to show us the next step.'

Now Haggard, Marshall and Anne Sloane had come quite close. Also Ras Tschubai, Ralf Marten and the robot. Rhodan was standing in their midst.

This was exactly the moment the invisible, mysterious mechanism seemed to have been waiting for. Very slowly, silently, the solid floor of the underground vault began to sink down. The rock walls appeared to slide upward. The seven men, Anne Sloane and the robot were standing on the platform of an elevator that kept steadily descending.

'Hope it'll turn out all right,' Bell muttered under his

breath. 'We should all have gotten off as long as the going was good. They certainly gave us plenty of time for that.'

'That was on purpose!' Rhodan remarked reproachfully. 'Haggard explained once that the immortal who intends passing on to us the secret of eternal life is not solely interested in how intelligent we are but also wants to make certain of our physical and psychic qualifications. This is just another test.'

Bell did not reply. Apparently he realized that Rhodan was right.

In the meantime the platform came to a standstill. Now the four rocky walls began to recede and the space, deep below the original vault, increased steadily in size. Suddenly a block came into sight, as if conjured up out of thin air. The block stood in the middle of the otherwise empty room.

A metal block.

Light came on. It was everywhere, in the walls, in the ceiling. The hall was cube-shaped, each side about ten yards long. The ceiling was now separating them from the shaft above. They were totally cut off from the outside world. Eight persons and a robot were sitting in a prison, in the most perfect trap.

The metal cube!

Their attention was at once drawn to it. Of course, for there was nothing else to be seen in this isolation cell.

Rhodan's probing eyes noticed that this cube showed the same well-known irregularities they had previously encountered.

The hieroglyphs and symbolic script of the immortals! They were clearly visible on the metal cube's side facing them. Was this inscription to be their next clue?

'How can we decipher these lines?' wondered Khrest. 'I have firmly anchored the symbols in my photographic memory. But how can we get to the positronic brain from here to decode the message? And how would we get back here again?'

Rhodan did not answer him directly. He simply turned around and motioned to the robot. The marvel of Arkonide technology reacted immediately. Markon came closer. Silently he waited for his orders.

'You see this inscription on the metal cube?' asked Rhodan.'

'Yes, sir.'

'Decode it and then let us have the text of that message.'

'Yes, sir.'

The robot focused his eyes, optical lenses, on the mysterious inscription. Then the robot, created in the image of his Arkonide builders, stood stockstill. Inside his metal body relays began to click. Contacts were made, new currents flowed into so-far unused regions of the small positronic brain. The inscription was photographed, then relayed to the proper parts of the brain to be decoded.

Bell showed impatience. 'Who knows if he'll succeed? And what will happen to us here in case he fails?'

'Worrywart!' It was John Marshall, disapproving loud and clear.

'What's that?'

'Cut it out!' ordered Rhodan. 'Let Markon get on with his work!'

In the background, Ras Tschubai and Ralf Marten carried on a whispered conversation. The teleporter was greatly tempted to try escaping their prison by simple dematerialization. But he did not dare to experiment without Rhodan's express command. After all, their prison chamber might be shut off from the outside world not merely by walls of rock but perhaps a time barrier or even a five-dimensional field. And these he could not penetrate.

The robot started to move. He turned around, fixing his rigid optical lens-eyes directly on Rhodan's face. 'The inscription was easy to decode. Here is the message: *Now seek out the man whose name you know. Only he possesses what you need in order to find the way to the Light. Do you know the meaning of time?*'

The robot fell silent. Rhodan waited a moment before he inquired: 'Is that all there is to the message?'

'That's the text of the entire inscription on the time-transformer, sir.'

Rhodan felt thunderstruck. His heart skipped beats, once, twice, three times. Then the blood streamed with renewed force back to his heart. He shuddered.

'What did you say, Markon? What is that over there?'

Rhodan pointed to the metal block in front of them.

The robot answered unemotionally: 'A time-transformer, sir. An instrument capable of manipulating the fourth and fifth dimensions. It serves the same purpose in fifth-dimensional mathematics as a computer does in three-dimensional calculations.'

'What can be accomplished with such a time-transformer, Markon?'

Bell, who had pressed forward, seemed to detect a trace of irony in the usually dispassionate voice of the robot.

'Transform time, sir. What else?'

'The joke's on us. That tin can is making fun of us!' Bell commented furiously. 'It pretends a time-transformer is nothing more than an abacus for little kids to learn to add and subtract.'

'Shut up, Reg!' Rhodan snapped at his friend. It was rare that he lost his temper. 'And if you have something to add to the discussion then make sure it will be something helpful, otherwise keep quiet.'

Rhodan again addressed the robot: 'You said the machine's purpose is to transform time? Does that mean this block is a time machine?'

'You might call it that, if you wish, sir. But a time-transformer is different from normal time machines. You cannot step into it and then travel forward or backward in time to whatever era you select. A transformer is set specifically for one certain date. It will take you to this time and then back again to the present. I am theoretically acquainted with the transformer's working principle.'

'Which direction will this transformer take?'

'Into the past, sir.'

Khrest had stepped up to Rhodan. 'Things are getting clearer now, Perry. Up there while you were sitting in that chair, the immortal ascertained that you knew the name of the Arkonide commander. As a result, we were permitted access to the time-transformer. There is no objection against bringing along your friends. Now this machine will carry us back in time, to give us the opportunity to meet Kerlon. For, according to the message, Kerlon is the one who possesses what will show us the path to the Light. Whatever this unknown thing might be, we don't know yet. We'll have to find it and then take it away from him.'

Bell and the mutants kept staring silently at the metal cube. It was a weird sensation to think that this inconspicuous looking metal piece should be able to transport them ten thousand years back into the past. Only the robot, incapable of experiencing emotions, remained undisturbed. Quietly it awaited whatever might come next.

'How does this transformer function, how can it be activated?' Rhodan looked inquiringly at Khrest. 'I can't find any controls.'

The robot reacted at once and answered in place of Khrest: 'The time-transformer is connected to the automatic mechanism in the vault. Our path has been preset. We cannot influence it in any way. I would say that we are already traveling backward in time.'

Startled, Rhodan looked around the room. The others reacted similarly. Nothing seemed to have changed in their temporary prison. They must still be somewhere underneath the vault of the Thort's Red Palace.

Or maybe not?

But before they could continue with their deliberations, something strange happened. Rhodan, Khrest, Bell and several of the mutants had already experienced it when they were in the hall of machines during the first stage of the galactic riddle. As before, they were seized once more by a sensation resembling horror, when the immortal's voice, preserved across thousands of years, spoke to them again out of the void.

It was a voice without sound, a mute, urging voice, that penetrated directly into the group's minds and therefore needed no translation.

It was a new message:

'I am speaking to the one who has followed my trail this far. When you arrive, be on guard; don't let yourself get killed. No one will come to your assistance; you must help yourself. And only if you find Kerlon, and with him that which will show you the way to the Light, will you be able to return to your own time. Wait for a period of exactly three days, not more nor less. Only then will the machine bring you back again. I hope you will succeed in this task. I have been waiting for such a long time already!'

From the distance they could suddenly hear vague noises. Rhodan thought he recognized shouts and screams, intermingled with the clanging of arms, as if people were fighting each other with swords. From somewhere came the roar of an explosion.

The walls of the dungeon began to change.

The smooth rock surfaces gave way to roughly hewn boulders. Over to the side where the entrance to the crypt had been could be seen a crude wooden door, locked from the inside by a heavy bolt. Floor and ceiling, however, remained the same.

The time-transformer stood in the same place as before. Nothing had changed there.

The noise grew stronger outside. Yelling and screaming mingled with new explosions. Shouted commands

58

could be heard from close by. Metal crashed on metal.

'I'm afraid,' said Khrest, 'we landed right in the middle of some altercation. According to our records, Ferrol was torn by strife at that time – today, rather. If indeed we're now in the past, we must count on getting involved in these battles.'

'Don't let yourself be killed – those were the immortal's warning words,' reminded Rhodan. 'I'm glad we thought of taking along some weapons.'

'Not enough, as far I'm concerned,' complained Bell, stroking the handle of his Arkonide pulse-ray gun. 'We should have brought along our special Arkonide protective suits, the psycho-ray gun, perhaps also the gravity-nullifier.'

'Even old-fashioned magazine rifles would be enough here to keep whole armies at bay.' Rhodan sounded rather confident. 'They're hardly acquainted with fire-arms yet, at best, some muzzle-loaders. Our ray guns should do the trick to prevent potential enemies from doing us in. But we must defend our lives at all costs. After all, we'll be fighting against people who have been long since dead. Ten thousand years ago, that's a long time! It seems weird to me!'

'Absolutely crazy! Spooky!' agreed Bell.

The battle noise outside grew weaker. It seemed to move away.

'We have three days,' Rhodan said in a matter-of-fact tone. 'I don't know if our watches are right but it should now be five o'clock in the afternoon according to Earth time. We have three days. I don't know at what time we arrived here but I'm confident that the immortal will have arranged matters in such a way that we'll have sufficient opportunity to look for Kerlon and to meet him. What I'm supposed to tell this commander of the Arkonides is still rather foggy. Khrest, do you have any suggestions?'

The Arkonide scientist slowly shook his head. 'Nothing is known in our history of a successfully executed trip through time. Since Kerlon sent his report from Venus, which he reached after having been on Ferrol, and since he didn't mention anything about having encountered human beings or Arkonides coming from the future, it stands to reason that we didn't tell him anything about it . . . or rather we aren't going to do so.'

'We'll see. Reg, open that door!'

It was easy to push back the bolt. The door swung open to the outside. Very little daylight came through the narrow window slots. Wide stone steps led upstairs, ending in a wide corridor. It was brightly lit by sunlight.

Three men in shining suits of armor were lying on the floor. Rhodan saw at once that they were dead. A terrible fight must have taken place here recently.

'Unpleasant chronological era.' Bell was visibly shaken. Cautiously he pulled his ray gun from his belt. With his thumb he adjusted it to weak intensity. This way a direct hit would mean a most unpleasant electrical shock without killing the victim.

Marshall had drawn his handgun too. He never went without it.

'Ras, you check out the lay of the land. Be careful – disappear the moment you meet anybody. Find out who the occupants of the Red Palace are and especially if the fleet of the three Arkonide ships has landed already. We'll wait here for your return.'

The African teleporter loosened the gun in his belt and started concentrating. The others watched in fascination as his figure grew hazy and finally vanished. They knew that he was rematerializing the same instant somewhere above in the Red Palace.

Waiting for his return was a nerve-racking affair.

Ras Tschubai had readied himself for a short jump.

Before he would rematerialize, he was unable to see where exactly this would take place. This had often resulted in dangerous situations for him. His only salvation had always been to take off immediately again for a new jump.

As he opened his eyes – he had concentrated on the throne room of the Thort – he started falling right away. Deep below he saw the towers and battlements of a low castle that bore no resemblance at all to the future Red Palace. Men in breastplates and armor stood at firing ports, firing away with heavy muskets at their enemies, who tried to storm the castle. Some enemy warriors were about to climb up ladders leaning against the heavy walls. Inside the courtyard there was hand-to-hand fighting. The attacking forces were about to overrun the defenders of the castle.

Ras could not waste any time, unless he wanted to crash to the ground. He dematerialized quickly and landed safely the same instant a mile away from the castle.

He set foot on the ground on a low hill. From here he could easily survey the surrounding area without risking detection by the barbarians.

He had an unimpeded view of the castle, which was besieged by a mighty army. In a little valley off to the side he could see the camp set up by the supply columns of the attackers. There were brightly burning camp fires; large animals were roasting on the spit. Primitive tents lined the banks of a little brook, well protected from the enemy's view by trees and bushes. Well-armed soldiers patrolled the entire area.

Ras heard some noises coming from behind. Quickly he turned around. The slightly undulating hill was overgrown with grass and occasional clumps of bushes that offered excellent cover to an approaching enemy.

There were four men trying to reach the summit, creeping close to the ground, avoiding any unnecessary noise. They wore no armor and this distinguished them immediately from the members of the two fighting parties.

Well, thought Ras to himself even then there were the so-called neutral forces who helped whichever party was victorious.

The four men wore leather jackets and narrow trousers of the same material. They were bareheaded but their long dark hair provided sufficient protection against heat or cold. Their arms consisted of long spears and short broadswords. Flat shields had been fastened to their backs with long leather belts.

Ras looked calmly in their direction. He was holding his ray gun in his hand. He was determined to disappear from the scene only in case of extreme emergency. He didn't want to return empty-handed to the cellar in the castle. Perhaps he could make himself understood with the few sentences of New-Ferronian he had learned back on Ferrol.

The four men were walking upright now, for they must have noticed that their attempts at concealment had failed. Filled with suspicion, they held their spears ready, while they still kept their hands off their swords. Their eyes expressed amazement at the oddly dressed stranger who looked at them without fear.

As soon as the four men had come within ten yards, Ras raised both hands.

'Stop!' He shouted to make sure they could hear him clearly. 'I want to talk with you.'

The four Ferrons halted. They seemed to have understood his words. Their spears were still held in their hands, ready to be thrown. They seemed puzzled; they didn't know what to make of this stranger. He belonged neither to the defenders nor to the attackers of the castle. Who could he be, then?

'Who are you?' asked a bushy-bearded Ferron.

Ras was astonished that he could understand him so well. This dialect differed only slightly from the way the Thort had spoken; it reminded him somewhat of the language used by the Sichas, the half-wild mountain tribes of Ferrol.

Could it be that he was confronting the forefathers of the Sichas here?

'Sicha?' Ras asked quickly.

The bearded man nodded his head, evidently rather puzzled. He lowered his spear gently until its point touched the ground. 'You – friend?' he wanted to know.

Now Ras in turn nodded yes in answer. After all, why shouldn't he be a friend of the Sichas? He pushed his ray gun back into his belt and walked toward the men, his bare hands stretched out to show his good intentions. Still he didn't forget to hold himself ready for an instantaneous jump in case the Sichas should undergo a sudden change of heart.

The bearded Sicha returned the gesture of friendship and firmly pressed the African's hand. The three other men, too, shook hands with him and quite openly expressed amazement at the strange looking weapon in his belt. Ras could fully appreciate their curiosity.

'We are living over there in the mountains,' the leader said, pointing to a mountain range far away on the horizon, only dimly visible in the haze. The setting sun was sinking closer to the mountaintops. 'Many wars now. We keep peace.'

'Who is making war?'

It turned out to be quite difficult for Ras to get the essential point of their confused explanation. The four men talked all at once, resorting occasionally to some local vernacular unknown to Ras. But finally he could piece together a picture of the situation.

The owner of the castle was a count, who ruled over this region. His neighbor, another count, challenged his claim to power. The current battle was the third attempt to wrest the castle from the rightful owner. The outcome of the fight seemed not to be in his favor. The Sichas did not directly join in the conflict but in their own way took advantage of it. They robbed the fallen warriors of their weapons and armor, or even attacked soldiers of either side who ventured out alone into the difficult terrain.

The bearded leader admitted this quite frankly and, when questioned by Ras why they did not try to rob him, grinned slyly and replied: 'You are a foreigner and wear strange clothing. You are armed with an odd-looking weapon different from those we possess. But we do know that your weapon can hurl bolts of lightning. We are afraid of you, therefore you are our friend.'

How amazingly simple and wise, thought Ras, startled by their logic. But then suddenly he was thunderstruck when he realized: how was it possible for these primitive Sichas to know that his ray gun could 'hurl bolts of lightning'?

The first landing of the immortals, long before the Arkonides! That must be it! The memory of this encounter must still be quite vivid in the minds of this primitive people.

'When was the last time that strangers visited your world?'

The bearded Sicha cocked his head. 'Are they your friends? Have you returned, Gods of the Sun?'

Ras pondered for a moment. Something didn't sound quite right. They weren't surprised by his black skin. Perhaps this wasn't remarkable in their eyes, for their complexion wasn't white either. They looked quite dark, almost bluish-black.

'Yes, they're my friends. They might return again.'

The bearded Sicha was just about to reply, when all were startled by wild yelling and warlike hollering.

The fierce shouts came from some nearby bushes that suddenly were teeming with life. At least one dozen soldiers, in full battle armor, jumped up at a shouted command and rushed toward the five men, who were completely taken by surprise.

The soldiers made no attempt to ask the obviously helpless men to surrender. All signs indicated clearly that they were not interested in taking them alive and making them their prisoners. For a few seconds Ras was determined to save his neck by a fast teleport-jump but then he thought better of it: it would have been most unfair to his newly won friends. After all, it was his fault that they had been trapped in this unfortunate situation.

Resolutely, he jerked his ray gun from his belt, while the Sichas, hurled their spears toward the enemy, drawing their swords a split second later.

Ras pressed the firing button, pointing the gun at the nearest opponent. The soldier had advanced toward them to within nearly twenty yards. He was just about to throw his spear at Ras when he was suddenly hit by the electron showers. His face distorted in a fierce grimace; he started screaming as if he were attacked by a whole company of soldiers. His fingers spread apart; his weapon dropped to the ground. Then he threw himself on the earth and began to beg for mercy.

His companions hesitated for a moment. Then, assuming that their comrade had probably been seized by some cramp, they proceeded with their attack. Brandishing their swords, they advanced toward their intended victims.

In the meantime, the Sichas' spears had found their

targets. Four of the attacking soldiers were hit and fell down. The rest of the enemy, however, had managed to aim their spears in the direction of Ras and the four Sichas. Suddenly, one of the Sichas next to the bearded leader uttered a scream and, pierced by the enemy's weapon, he sank into the grass.

Now Ras's patience finally came to an end.

He immediately changed the intensity of his ray gun and directed the ray nonstop against the six or seven remaining opponents who, swords drawn, were racing closer and closer to the apparently helpless group. The soldiers' fierce faces left no doubt what fate they had in mind for them.

The enemy's attack stopped short of its goal. The soldiers appeared to run full force into an invisible wall and bounce back violently. Their horrified cries rent the air; their swords dropped to the ground. Their limbs stiffened, as if seized by cramps, then, suddenly, they slumped helplessly into the grass.

They were not dead but Ras was convinced that they had been knocked out completely for the next half hour. Only the first soldier, who had been hit by the initial weak electron shower, jumped up from where he had been lying begging for mercy and ran downhill, screaming in sheer horror.

The bearded leader of the Sichas in the meantime had picked up a spear, ready to send it off in the direction of the fleeing soldier. With a pacifying gesture Ras placed his hand on the man's arm. 'Let him get away, my friend!'

'Why? He'll get other soldiers to finish us off.'

'I don't believe he'll get reinforcements. He'll tell his

67

comrades what's happened here – then no one will have the courage to come out to this hill anymore. It's safer here than over there in the castle that will soon be taken by the enemy.'

This seemed to make sense to the Sichas.

'It's time, anyway, for us to leave,' their leader said. 'Otherwise we won't manage to reach our mountains. Soon God's Eye will sink below the earth and it will become dark.'

'God's Eye?' Ras asked, astonished, but in the same instant he realized that they had meant the sun by this. 'Why, of course, soon night will fall. Describe exactly where your homes are so that I can visit you later.'

'You aren't coming along with us?' The bearded man's voice revealed his disappointment.

'No, I'm sorry, but my friends are waiting for me. I must return to them. But I promise you that I'll visit you someday. Just tell me how to find the way to your home.'

The leader looked over to the far horizon, then pointed to an especially high mountaintop. 'Over there, beyond the triangle mountain, is where my tribe is living. A high plateau, next to a wide valley with a stream. You can't miss it.'

I most certainly won't, thought Ras, for the Sicha had described the exact spot where later on would rise Sic-Horum, their capital city.

'I'll find it. Get home safely.'

The Sicha smiled broadly. 'We know many secret paths that are unknown to soldiers from foreign lands. Farewell, stranger. And – thanks.'

Ras shook hands with the three brave warriors and

68

pushed his ray gun back into his holster. He knew what surprise awaited these semi-savages. He only regretted that he would be unable to observe their perplexed faces when he suddenly vanished into thin air right in front of them.

A final wave to his friends. Then he concentrated on the cellar underneath the castle – and jumped.

He opened his eyes and peered into Bell's frightened face.

4. THE GODS INTERVENE

The ruler of the castle, and district Thorta, recognized that his resistance was in vain. The barbarians had penetrated into the fortress and threatened to overcome the rest of his soldiers who were still alive.

He summoned the captain of the soldiers. 'Regor, gather up your men. We're withdrawing into the vaults below the castle. We'll be able to hold out there for a few more days.'

'The enemy has already advanced as far as the cellars, Lesur,' answered the captain. 'But we succeeded in killing them. Wouldn't it be better to seek refuge in the secret chamber?'

Lesur raised his hand in protest. 'The secret chamber is a holy shrine. No mortal may ever see its interior without losing his life immediately. No, the other cellars will have to do. I have sufficient food stored there. Our women are there already. Order your men to withdraw at once. If we remain up here we'll all be lost.'

Regor saluted and hurried to his soldiers.

Lesur, however, one of the many Thorts of Ferrol, stormed toward the wide, roughly hewn stone stairway leading below. Outside, in the courtyard, his troops were battling with the enemy invaders. The war was lost; the barbarians were winning. The end of civilization had come. Slavery and barbarism would be the rule from now on.

The heavy door leading to the vaults in the basement was smashed. Heavy fighting must have taken place here, for the wood had been splintered by mighty sword thrusts and heavy clubs.

Lesur hesitated a moment. The battle noise coming from the pinnacles seemed to grow louder. In all probability the barbarians had succeeded in scaling the walls. There was little chance that Regor and his men could save themselves in time.

There was precious little time left now for himself.

He hurried down the steps, ran through long corridors and passed the first guard post. The enemy had not penetrated this far. And most likely would not do so for quite a while. The narrow window slots below the ceiling were too small to permit passage to any enemy soldier.

The women and old men looked up as Lesur entered the wide hall through the heavy wooden door. Soldiers were standing to the left and right of the entrance. The children stopped in their play. The noise of the battle could only vaguely be heard from here. No one down here knew what fate had in store for the castle and their own lives. The Thort decided to tell them the full truth.

But he wanted to wait with it until Regor and his soldiers could join them down here. Then the door would be locked tight. They would be safe as long as their provisions would last. This was as much as they had been able to do. Unless some miracle would save them from this underground prison.

A soldier stormed through the door, saw Lesur and stumbled toward him. He sank to his knees. The Thort observed that the man was trembling all over.

'What's going on? What's happened?' the Thort snapped at the desperate man. 'You needn't fear telling me the truth. There can be nothing worse than the news I know of already.'

The man raised his head. Tears were streaming from his eyes, running down his cheeks. 'Oh, Lord, the Gods . . .'

'If only they'd come to our help!' Lesur said sarcastically and turned away. There was no time now to devote to the religious comfort of his soldiers. The Gods had forsaken him; therefore, as far as he was concerned, they could stay wherever they might be now.

'But, they're going to help us!' shouted the soldier, rising. 'They've heard our prayers and they'll come to our assistance. Why else would they have come here?'

Lesur's body grew rigid. 'Come here? Who's come here?'

'The Gods! They're already inside the castle. I've just seen one of them as I was praying outside the holy chamber. The door was open. . . .'

'What are you telling me?' yelled Lesur, horrified. 'The door is open? Have you seen this with your own eyes?'

'Oh yes, Lord, the door was open. I know that it's been closed since time immemorial. Everyone knows that it must never be opened. They say the Gods are living behind that door and they come out from there in the time of greatest need. Now they've opened that door. The Gods have come to help us.'

For a few seconds Lesur stood stockstill. Then he

seized the soldier's arm and snapped at him: 'Come with me! We're going to the door of the Gods!'

Bell was scared to death when Ras suddenly materialized right in front of him. He cursed and stepped back quickly.

The African chuckled in amusement. Then he reported to the impatiently waiting group about the situation outside, as far as he had been able to observe it.

'We didn't travel back in time,' began Rhodan thoughtfully, 'to interfere in the inner politics of the Ferronian tribes. I must admit, though, that I prefer the Thort of this castle to the attacking barbarians. We're now confronted by the question: what should we do now? As far as Ras has found out, the Arkonides haven't yet landed here on Ferrol.'

This time it was Anne Sloane who suggested a plan, demonstrating that women, too, can think logically. 'In case these barbarians conquer the castle, we're threatened by a great danger. There will hardly be any chance that these savages will spare our lives, if it is their custom to kill anything in sight. We should try perhaps to ingratiate ourselves with the master of this castle. Then we can sit and wait here calmly until the Arkonides land here.'

'That's a splendid suggestion,' agreed Ras. 'There's still another possibility: we can wait for the Arkonides' arrival in the safety of the Sichas' settlements.'

'Getting there without the proper means of transportation would be too complicated,' Rhodan objected. 'Anne's plan seems to make sense.'

Reginald Bell's face lit up. 'Great! We're going to

defend the castle! We'll just mingle unobtrusively with the knights!'

Rhodan laughed. 'Unobtrusively? Hardly! I'm afraid we'll scare those knights out of their wits.'

Khrest wanted to add something but he suddenly began to listen intently. He remained silent.

There was some noise coming from the outside. The door was still standing open, and they could clearly hear steps that were cautiously approaching. Two men were talking to each other.

Rhodan motioned to the mutants. Weapons drawn, the three men and the young girl moved silently to the back of the room. Khrest and Rhodan remained near the door. The exciting moment of the first contact with men from the past was imminent.

What would the reaction be?

But it turned out quite different from what they had feared.

Upon seeing the open door, Lesur realized that his soldier had spoken the truth. He was seized by an inexplicable awe and regretted the snide remarks he'd made not too long ago regarding the Gods. Would they still forgive him for this? He decided to behave especially humble.

He saw three men. They were standing in front of a metal cube in the center of the bare room. The awe-inspiring figures of the three forced Lesur down on his knees. His soldier had already prostrated himself, lying trembling with fear on the stone floor.

Rhodan didn't understand right away. From the back wall, where John Marshall was standing, came a tele-pathic message. John could read the minds of the

Ferrons and he transmitted his thoughts to the uncomprehending Rhodan: 'He believes us to be Gods who've come in order to help him against the barbarians. Right now he's still deliberating how he should address us. I think his Ferronian dialect won't be too difficult for us to understand. His name is Lesur, the Thort.'

Rhodan sized up the situation. He stepped forward and halted at the threshold of the door. Before Lesur could utter a word, Rhodan stretched out both hands toward the Ferron and addressed him in the New-Ferronian language:

'You've guessed it, Lesur. We've come to help you. We won't permit your enemies to conquer your castle.'

Lesur understood the words, although they seemed to be strangely altered. But this wasn't surprising: why shouldn't the Gods speak differently from mere mortals? The important thing was that he could comprehend what they were telling him.

Lesur rose from his knees but still remained with head and shoulders bowed down in a deferential attitude.

'Thank you, O Gods! But the enemy has already invaded my castle. Many warriors have been killed and now women and children are in danger of sharing their fate.'

Hearing of the immediate danger threatening the women and children caused Rhodan to act faster than he had intended. He turned to his friends: 'Bell, take charge of the cleaning-up operation of the inner castle, together with Khrest and the robot. I'll occupy myself with the defense on the outside. Marten, Ras, Marshall and Anne Sloane will come with me. Reg, follow the usual procedure: ray guns, slight intensity. The mutants and I will take care of the barbarians. I'll put the fear of God into those savages. That can never do any harm.'

Lesur and his soldier led Bell and his three companions in the direction of the great hall where a battle was already raging. Rhodan and his mutants, however, hurried up the stone stairs to the observation platform from where they wanted to survey the situation. They encountered the first barbarians already in the courtyard. The rest of the defenders had fled to the corridors leading to the cellar vaults. The intruders thought themselves to be conquerors.

And now suddenly these strangers appeared before them.

Surrounded by his chieftains, Gagat, ruler of the barbarians, saw the new opponents.

He wasted no time in finding out what these strangers wanted from him. It quickly passed through his mind that Lesur must have acquired some new allies from some distant land – and he ordered his soldiers to kill these men.

Rhodan held his ray gun ready in his hand.

'What's going on?' he whispered to Marshall.

The telepath replied hastily: 'They regard us as enemies. The fellow with the red cape is their leader – he's called Gagat. He just issued a command to his soldiers to kill us.'

'That's it,' Rhodan said. 'Now we know where we stand. Let's go, then! Everyone proceed to the best of their abilities. I'll use the ray gun. Anne, why don't you let this Gagat rise up into the air for a little while!'

But it took several minutes before Anne could let Gagat fly like a bird. There was no time, for she had to concentrate her attention first on steering aside the enemy's missiles. She used her telekinetic talents with great skill and incredible presence of mind. The result of her endeavors was a smashing success.

The leader of the barbarians raised his spear and hurled it toward Rhodan, whom he might have recognized as the most important person among these enemies. The missile was well aimed and would have hit Rhodan without fail if it had not bounced in midair against some invisible obstacle. For a moment the spear remained there motionless, then arched backward, returning to its starting point. However, with the identical speed. The barbarian stared wide-eyed at this miracle and could not even muster enough energy to dodge his own spear, that now landed almost straight down, nailing his right root to the hard loam of the courtyard.

He uttered a piercing scream, due mainly to fear rather than pain. Gagat, who was standing next to him, had not budged. He was busy watching the other soldiers' spears that performed the most peculiar acrobatics. Some rose up so high into the air that he almost lost sight of them. Others changed their flight path and hit against the stone walls of the fortress with such force that missiles broke in two. None, however, reached their intended goal.

Rhodan, meanwhile, had pointed his ray gun at the dumbfounded barbarians and directed a slight electron shower at them. Filled with fury, Gagat seized his sword, ready to lead his warriors with a good example, when the black ghost of the African suddenly materialized next to him, calmly took away his sword and vanished again without a trace.

The savage stood there thunderstruck.

And then the electric current began to course through his body. He was totally unfamiliar with this type of energy. His soldiers' terrified faces told him that he was not alone in experiencing this frightening phenomenon.

Who were these strangers?

Before he could come to a conclusion, one of them spoke to him. Gagat could even understand what he was saying.

'Gagat, return to your land or the Gods will kill you and your men. To show you that we mean business, here is a last demonstration and our final warning.'

Rhodan gave Anne Sloane a sign, and she started concentrating on Gagat. Then the most frightening event for Gagat began.

The leader of the barbarians felt suddenly how the painful tingling ceased in his body, but at the same time he lost the firm ground from under his feet. He floated upward, higher and higher, until he reached the highest pinnacles of the castle. His eyes almost popping out of their sockets in terror, his legs dangling like two lifeless sticks, he kept rising up like a balloon. For a while he hovered above the fiercely battling warriors of both sides, who fought for possession of the watch tower. At first he remained unnoticed but then someone called out.

All eyes turned skyward and then all arms, with swords and spears raised up high to do battle, sank down helplessly. Gagat, the feared and pitiless barbarian, could fly like a bird.

What a shock for Lesur's soldiers! But this lasted only a few seconds, for by that time they had noticed the barbarians' reaction to their leader's remarkable feat: they were just as horrified as the castle's defenders.

Gagat, too, gave himself away. As he hovered close above the soldiers' head, he started calling out to them:

'The Gods are on Lesur's side! They've lifted me up into the sky and soon they'll let me fall down to the ground. Give up the fight; we've lost! We cannot prevail against the Gods.'

Marshall, down in the courtyard, could weakly hear Gagat's words. He turned to Ralf Marten, the tele-optician, and said: 'Ralf, establish contact with Gagat. See what's happening to him!'

The tall, dark-haired halfbreed Japanese withdrew to the nearest wall of the courtyard and leaned against the stones. Here it would be safe to leave his body for a short while. Rhodan would take care that no one would come too close as long as he was in this helpless condition.

A moment later he could perceive through Gagat's eyes. He peered into the horrified faces of the barbarians and into the once more hopeful features of Lesur's men. He could also hear as the lord of the barbarians shouted anew: 'Flee, as long as there's still time. Maybe the wrath of the Gods will spare me if we obey their command. Leave Lesur's castle as fast as you can!'

Ralf Marten returned into his body; he had heard enough. Rhodan looked at him expectantly.

'I think we scared them sufficiently,' Marten said, smiling.

The barbarians fled helter-skelter. They paid no heed to the electron showers. They drew their swords from their sheaths and stormed toward the castle walls to reach the ladders that had enabled them some time ago to scale the same walls. Desperately they pushed and shoved, trying to reach safety first. More than one of the ladders toppled over, hurtling the men down to their deaths.

Up at the watch tower sheer pandemonium reigned. Lesur's furious soldiers wanted to prevent the barbarians' flight; they intended to take full revenge on the suddenly weakened enemy. Meanwhile Gagat, who was still floating close above the fighting men, kept violently waving his arms in the air. This caused him to sail nearer to the edge of the castle walls and then beyond, until he hung above the sheer void.

The ground lay deep below him. If he should crash now, his life would be lost.

But Anne had no intention whatsoever of killing him. She let him descend swiftly, braking just in time for him to land gently, not far beyond the castle moat. Gagat stood there all alone and observed, still half-paralyzed with fright, the flight of his panic-stricken braves.

Gradually the survivors gathered around their leader. They still failed to comprehend how Gagat could suddenly fly through the air – but if the Gods, especially hostile ones, were involved, one had to expect such incredible happenings.

Still missing were those soldiers who had invaded the interior of the castle. Would they manage to flee the wrath of Lesur's men or were they lost? There was no time left to find out now. Gagat and his men fled head over heels.

Rhodan didn't hinder them in their flight. He waited until some of Lesur's soldiers appeared. As was to be expected, there were no complications; Gagat's words had done their work. The Gods had interfered and helped them to win the victory. Now it was proper to thank the Gods.

It was not surprising, therefore, that Rhodan and his friends found themselves soon circled by a group of kneeling Ferrons, who touched their foreheads to the ground in order to show their reverence and gratitude.

What a pity, thought Rhodan, *that Reg isn't here to witness this spectacle . . .*

In the meantime Reginald Bell was busy warding off the attacking barbarians with the help of positron ray guns. This task, however, did not prove quite as easy perhaps as Rhodan had thought.

Lesur and his warriors hurried ahead and stopped abruptly when they reached the corridor that ended in the entrance to the sanctuary. Just five minutes earlier calm and peace had reigned here. But now all hell had broken loose!

Regor, chieftain of the Ferrons, had sent down some of his soldiers into the cellar vaults in order to prepare and orderly withdrawal. As they passed through the throne chamber, they had encountered some barbarian invaders, who had already begun to plunder. Violent fighting had ensued, which saw the rightful owners of the castle being pushed back farther and farther.

Now they were waging a desperate fight to prevent the enemy from taking their last refuge, that hall where women and children were hidden.

Bell sized up the situation at once.

'Continuous fire!' he ordered Khrest and Haggard. Bell himself pointed his weapon at the battling men and pressed the firing button. It was impossible to distinguish friend from foe. Thus both Ferrons and barbarians were seized by the electron showers. Bell had set the gun on purpose for a higher intensity and it did not take long before some of the soldiers, clad in metal armor, received rather strong electrical shocks.

The walls of the vault were reverberating with cries of sheer horror.

Lesur shouted a few words to explain the situation to his men. Though they could not understand why the Gods would apparently punish them too, they obeyed Lesur's command and disentangled themselves from their foes and retreated in the direction of the sanctuary. Some of Lesur's men were unable to walk; they barely managed to crawl.

In the meantime the barbarians recovered from their fright.

Strangers had appeared, holding oddly-shaped objects in their hands. Then they felt these unknown electrical shocks, which were most unpleasant but not particularly painful.

Bogar himself gave the order to attack these

strangers. He brandished his sword and advanced toward Bell.

Man can manufacture robots but these will always remain the work of mere mortals. The robots carry out man's commands. They are incapable of independent thought for they lack intelligence.

It was quite a different story as far as Arkonide robots were concerned. They were equipped with a brain capable of independent thought processes. They needed no instructions in order to react to danger. They acted on individual initiative for they had the same discerning powers as their creators.

Markon the robot stood next to Bell. He saw that his master was about to be attacked. Therefore he acted accordingly.

Bogar hesitated for a moment when he saw the stranger come toward him. Properly speaking, this stranger was the only one who did not impress him as alien as the others, for he wore a suit of armor like Bogar and his men. How should the barbarian know that Markon was constructed entirely of metal?

A true opponent, thought Bogar. But how odd that he did not carry arms. Did he intend, perhaps, to defend himself with his bare fists against a sword?

Bogar no longer paid heed to Bell; he turned and concentrated his attention on the robot who now was advancing toward him with arms outstretched.

Bell watched the scene out of the corners of his eyes. He had to continue covering the barbarians with his ray gun.

Bogar, protected by his heavy suit of armor, raised his sword with both hands and with all his might he brought it down swiftly upon Markon's head. The force of the impact would have cut in half any ordinary helmet. Even a shield would not have helped there. Instead the barbarian's sword simply twisted and became nothing more than a useless piece of iron. At the same time Bogar broke both wrists. Roaring with pain he dropped the now worthless weapon and sank to his knees. Tears of pain and anger rolled down his cheeks. All the while he kept staring at the marvelous warrior who had proved to be invulnerable.

Markon turned, ignoring Bogar. With automatic precision he walked on, right into the path of the bunched rays of the positron pistols shielding himself from their effect. He proceeded toward one of the soldiers and with one jerky movement took away his half-raised sword. With the flat side of the blade he hit the man in the small of the back. The soldier began to stagger but caught himself in time before he hit the ground and raced off screaming at the top of his voice.

Now two other barbarians made a decision. The choice was not difficult – as far as they were concerned. Either they would give up the fight and perish or they would try to defend themselves and have at least a sporting chance to reach safety.

Resolutely they attacked Markon. Bell, who still kept surveying the scene, noticed with surprise how excellent and skillful a fighter Markon turned out to be. This was, of course, also due to the most efficient protection of his Arkonite body hull. The sword blows bounced off the metal without leaving as much as a dent. On the other hand, Markon's first two mighty blows smashed the barbarians' armor to pieces. Sparks were flying as the thin iron sheeting was being cut to ribbons. Both barbarians fled in panic, immediately to be joined by the rest of the soldiers in their headlong flight.

'The Gods are on our side!' shouted Lesur to the fleeing enemy and simultaneously this stopped his own men who were so scared that they were about to follow suit.

'Cease fire!' yelled Bell to his friends. Bogar was taken prisoner. Markon carefully placed the damaged sword on a stone ledge and said to Bell:

'A most interesting way of fighting. A certain skill seems indispensable for it.'

Khrest intervened: 'Markon, you know you have some vulnerable spots! If they would have been accidentally hit by a blow with the soldiers' swords you would have been finished.'

'He had to run that risk,' Bell defended the robot, who seemed to become increasingly sympathetic to him by the minute.

Meanwhile Lesur reached the entrance to the hall. He announced the Gods' victory over the barbarians who had been sent fleeing for their lives. Indescribable scenes of rejoicing followed. Shouting and yelling triumphantly, women and children surged out into the corridor and prostrated themselves before Bell and Markon. Khrest and Haggard stayed in the background, observing the scene with mixed emotions. In the midst of an adoring crowd stood Bell and Markon, a human being and a creature consisting of metal and positronic circuitry. From somewhere came Bogar's pitiful whining. From up above the clanging of arms could still be heard. The Ferrons were chasing out the enemy.

Lesur exited from the hall, approached Bell and sank to his knees in front of him. With an imploring gesture he lifted his arms.

'Praise the mighty Gods! Our eternal gratitude is yours! We were certain that you would come to our assistance in our hour of need. The enemy has been defeated. Now tell us your price! We will pay whatever you demand!'

Bell racked his brains. What would Rhodan say in his place? What after all was the reason for their coming here?

The spaceships of the Arkonide expedition ten thousand years ago! That's why they had traveled back in time!

'Noble Lesur,' Bell began cautiously, 'no special tribute is needed. But we plan to to stay here with you for several days. We're waiting to welcome our friends who soon will arrive from out of the skies. Then we'll depart again.'

'Friends from the skies?' Lesur stammered in awe. 'So you'll go back again into the locked chamber?'

'Yes, back into the secret room,' replied Bell and glanced down on the bowed heads at his feet.

And he emitted a deep, deep sigh.

What a pity, he thought, *that Rhodan isn't here to witness this spectacle.*

5. TIME TURNED BACK

Two days had gone by.

The members of the time traveling expedition were still staying in the reconquered castle as guests of the Ferronian count. Busily scurrying servants brought food, drink and anything else they needed. Meanwhile, Ras Tschubai had locked the chamber with the time machine from the inside to prevent any unauthorized persons from entering. Rhodan did not wish to forfeit their only path back to present time.

A talk with Lesur had reassured Rhodan that the Arkonides would not be the first space travelers to land on Ferrol.

'Many summers and winters ago,' the count reported in a mysterious tone, 'the first Gods descended from the skies. Our forefathers came to their assistance. As a reward they received those peculiar gifts that are still to be seen all over the country. Down below in my castle's cellars is also one of these cages. No one is permitted to come close to it for we have lost the knowledge of how to use them properly. Many courageous men who entered that cage have vanished from sight, never to return.'

'They didn't come back?' Rhodan asked, puzzled. He could communicate quite passably with the precursor of the later Thort but there were still many things he could not comprehend. It was obvious that the Ferrons of this particular era had not yet figured out the significance of the matter transmitters. Ensuing centuries or thousands of years would probably have to pass before they would acquire the necessary knowledge and insight.

'Nearly all failed to return,' Lesur said. 'A strange story. He was a scientist. He entered the cage down in the cellar and moved the lever. Then he vanished. Not until two years later did he reappear in the castle, disheveled and starved. He claimed to have wandered halfway around our planet; but he couldn't explain how he had ever gotten to the other side of the world.'

It'll take a long time, Rhodan thought to himself, before these half-savages will be able to understand teleportation. It would be premature to try to enlighten them. Besides, it was none of his business to do so. The transmitters, however, interested him very much indeed.

'May I see this apparatus?'

'The box cage?' Lesur hesitated. He seemed to fear that the Gods who had saved them from destruction might disappear in it. 'If you insist on it; my Lord. . . .'

'We're well acquainted with these instruments,' Rhodan reassured the count. 'And if I vanish in it, I promise you to return soon.'

Rhodan risked the jump on the afternoon of the second day. He rematerialized somewhere in the middle of the night. The transmitter had indeed transported him around to the other side of Ferrol. As far as he could make out in the darkness, the matter receiver-transmitter was located in some kind of a temple on a mountaintop, all alone and abandoned. A forgotten shrine of past generations.

It was not forgotten after all. Hardly had Rhodan materialized when shadowy figures moved among the stone walls of the dilapidated temple. Silently they closed in on him. Their hands brandished glittering swords. In the faint glow of the stars Rhodan recognized flowing robes.

Priests!

He did not hesitate. Immediately he activated the sending mechanism of the transmitter and stood again in the cellar of the castle in front of the baffled Lesur.

Lost in thought, Rhodan went to the group's quarters. His conjectures had been confirmed. The immortals had provided the savage Ferrons with a grandiose transportation system all over Ferrol. But the gift's purpose had remained a mystery for the half-savage tribes. Here inside the castle the transmitter stood unused, while on the other side of the planet it was jealously guarded by suspicious priests.

No doubt all who had dared the leap into the unknown had been murdered, all except the scientist.

On the morning of the third day the three ships of the Arkonides touched down on Ferrol.

Commander Kerlon's resemblance to Khrest was only superficial.

This epoch's Arkonides showed no sign yet of any degeneration. The race was still at the height of its development. The galactic empire was flourishing and grew larger with each successful expedition.

And Kerlon knew that he was on the track of the most fantastic mystery – immortality, eternal life!

Somewhere in this section of the galaxy there was a

planet that was the home of a race that had discovered the secret of cell rejuvenation. Kerlon's expedition had detected clues pointing to this secret during several landings on planets throughout the galaxy.

All signs pointed to this system, as well as to another one that was twenty-seven light-years distant. A yellow star with nine planets. One of these planets was characterized by a triple ring around it.

Kerlon had landed first on an uninhabited continent of the eighth planet of this system which had altogether forty-three planets. His choice to touch down on this particular world had been quite arbitrary. The rocky high plateau was devoid of any sign of life. Only the tall, four-cornered pyramid of some unknown metal revealed that some intelligent life-form must have preceded them here.

A thousand years ago? Or ten thousand years?

The pyramid was hollow and easily opened. Without delay Kerlon and some of his scientists entered. They were courageous and brave. They did not know fear. He acted automatically and unconsciously, by sheer instinct.

Kerlon found, deep below the surface, a small five-cornered room with a table. An object was lying on the table.

From the walls of the room came an even glow that made the object recognizable. It was as if the object itself was aglow but in reality it merely reflected the light from the surrounding walls.

A metallic cylinder. A hollow cylinder?

Kerlon's companions were apprehensive as their commander stepped forward to touch the object. What if the unknown's patience had finally come to an end? Had he not lured them now into a cleverly constructed trap?

But nothing of the sort happened. Kerlon picked up the cylinder. It was light and easy to handle about one foot long and four inches thick. There was a lid at one end but all attempts to unscrew it failed.

Impatiently, Kerlon returned to his spaceship. Most unwillingly he handed the cylinder over to his scientists. He felt deep satisfaction when they, too, fared no better than he had in trying to open it.

Once more Kerlon went back to the pyramid. But he found nothing of importance. Then one of his scientists detected in a side room an odd-looking cage. Kerlon noticed a lever inside. So he entered the cage and depressed the lever. Kerlon was one of those who never hesitated to risk their own life for the common good.

His companions were absolutely convinced that the unknowns would destroy him this time. Kerlon was bound to fall victim to their wrath. And when their commander vanished suddenly, they no longer had any doubt: they had lost their leader.

But Kerlon was not lost forever. Hardly ten seconds had passed before he reappeared, somewhat pale and frightened, but unharmed. The scientists were overjoyed and eagerly questioned him. Kerlon, however, only shook his head absentmindedly, and looked up at the sun, standing at high noon. Then he sat down on the nearest rock next to the entrance of the pyramid. He decided to break his silence.

'It is noon,' he began slowly. 'A few seconds ago it was darkest night, somewhere on the opposite side of this planet. That cage inside the pyramid is a matter transmitter. We have only theoretical knowledge of such an apparatus; we have never been able to build one. How is it possible that such a complicated instrument should exist here on this planet that is inhabited by primitive savages?'

No one could answer that question.

Kerlon realized that nobody on this world was even intelligent enough to comprehend the function of a matter transmitter. Let alone construct one. The Arkonides themselves must be quite inferior – at least from a technical point of view – to the builders of such matter transmitters. Therefore danger threatened their developing empire. They had finally encountered an opponent who had to be taken seriously. Unfortunately, no one knew who this opponent was and what he looked like.

This matter must be investigated! If the metal cylinder would not supply the answer, perhaps then the matter transmitters might. One of them had to lead them to their builders. All matter transmitters on this plane had therefore to be tried out.

A difficult task, considering that the natives might confront them either with awe and fear or with hostility. And the Arkonides thought it beneath them to enter into battles with inferior races. Not only that, it was strictly forbidden to do so This left not even the effective alternative of self-defense in case of an emergency.

It was just a matter of chance. Some of the natives regarded the spacefaring Arkonides as Gods while others opposed them as bitter enemies. Thus Kerlon knew he had to search for those natives who were inclined to look upon the spacemen as religious symbols.

Kerlon started out with his fleet and after a long search landed directly next to a castle built on the top of a small hill. The wide fields that stretched to the far horizon, where a mountain chain was faintly visible, showed signs of planned cultivation. At least halfway civilized intelligent beings must live here.

Kerlon's conclusion was correct but only partially. How could he guess that, hidden in the nearby woods, the barbarians were awaiting their chance to avenge their defeat. Gagat, having overcome his shock at having fought against the Gods, was also unknown to Kerlon, of course. Gagat had arrived at the conclusion that his dealings had not been with the Gods. These were no divine beings who had beaten them. The world was big and mighty warriors lived in it but they could be overcome by force rather than cleverness and ruses.

Gagat gathered up the survivors of his unsuccessful attack and lay in ambush in the woods near the castle. All he had to do was to wait for the time when the strangers would leave the castle, then he could easily wipe them out.

The barbarians were surprised no end then when early on the morning of the third day three gigantic silvery spheres appeared in the clear blue sky. These giant silver balls were much larger even than the sun, God's eye! The mysterious objects came closer and closer and finally softly touched down at quite some distance from where Gagat and his men lay hidden.

Gagat had to bring into play his utmost persuasiveness and authority to hold his warriors back from taking instantly to their heels. Who could blame the defeated soldiers if now they lost heart for good. Gods were occupying the castle and now reinforcements arrived from out of the skies. No one, not even the bravest warrior, could be expected to fight against such odds.

Gagat, however, thought differently. And the events that followed seemed to justify his point of view – at least to begin with.

When Rhodan and his friends learned about the three landed spaceships, they knew that they were definitely on the right track in their pursuit of the immortals,

Lesur himself brought them the good news. He was very excited. 'My Lord, they have arrived. Just as you predicted.'

Outwardly Rhodan kept calm while a storm was raging inside him. The Arkonides had come, the very same Arkonides who, ten thousand years ago, had flown into Earth's solar system to establish a base on the planet Venus.

Time had been turned back. Not until this moment had Rhodan been able to fully appreciate the significance of this event.

'Where have they landed, Lesur?'

'On the plain between the castle and the woods. Will you go out to welcome them?'

Rhodan looked questioningly at Khrest, who shook his head imperceptibly. Rhodan wondered why but did not inquire any further.

'We'll send some delegates to meet them. Wait outside near the gate.'

As soon as the Ferron had left, Rhodan glanced at Khrest. The Arkonide scientist smiled gently. 'We don't want to rouse Kerlon's suspicions needlessly. Besides, nothing has been noted in the central files on Arkon that Kerlon's expedition discovered representatives of the human race during his stay in the Vega system. I'll go myself.'

'Is that less suspicious?'

'Of course. At that time – ten thousand years ago – we had many Arkonide research ships exploring the known and unknown regions of our universe. They didn't necessarily keep in touch with each other. Therefore, Kerlon doesn't know me. I shall simply tell him that we landed here several months earlier and have thoroughly explored this planet and this solar system. Maybe I can persuade him to continue his flight, this time toward Earth.'

'Wouldn't that be . . .' Rhodan began but then his voice failed. He stared at Khrest with amazement. The Arkonide was still smiling.

'Yes, that would be an explanation why Kerlon arrived so fast at your solar system and kept searching there for such a long time for the planet of immortality, until he died unexpectedly. His suspicions seem to have become aroused later on but by then it was too late. In any case, he never admitted that a fellow Arkonide had led him around by the nose.'

'Are you trying to influence the course of the future?'

'No,' Khrest replied, 'I'm merely creating the proper conditions so that we'll find the right answers to our questions on Venus ten thousand years from now. Whatever you want to call that ...? I really wouldn't know.'

Rhodan did not answer, for what could he have said in reply to that puzzling statement?

Khrest was unusually active. Once again the old drive awakened in him, the drive that had enabled his race to build up a star realm. The long ensuing periods of inactivity and degeneration were forgotten now. Khrest had changed back into one of those Arkonides who had conquered entire solar systems and incorporated them with one swoop into their galactic empire.

Perhaps this transformation might be attributed to the fact that he was transposed to the Golden Age of Arkonide history – after all, nothing was really known about the psychological effects of time travel.

'I'll take Markon along with me,' said Khrest, checking the charge of his pulsator weapon. 'Robots of the same type were known at that time already.'

'And how about ray guns?' Rhodan inquired, hoping for once to have caught Khrest in a moment of carelessness. But the Arkonide scientist smiled indulgently and patted the butt of his weapon.

'It's the identical model we've been using for more than ten thousand years. This gun is absolutely perfect; why should we change it?' Then, turning to Marshall: 'I'm leaving now, Marshall; can you keep in contact with me?'

The telepath hesitated slightly before he answered: 'It will work out all right if I concentrate on you. I hope the distance between us won't be too great.'

'I'm sure you'll make it, Marshall.' Then Khrest looked at the robot and ordered: 'Accompany me!'

Rhodan watched as Khrest and the robot left. He felt uneasy. He hated to have to remain behind. For the first time the initiative had been wrested from his hands – by an argument of logic.

Kerlon was busy organizing a small expedition when he noticed three figures approaching his ship.

The three men were not dressed alike; they looked different from each other.

They came down from the castle and were now walking across the plain. In the lead was a silvery shimmering monster whose shape and movements seemed somewhat familiar to Kerlon. At first he thought it to be a man wearing a suit of armor but then he recognized it as a robot.

A robot? Here on this primitive world?

He turned to one of his officers. 'Switch on the visicope with the magnifier. I have the sinking feeling we've arrived here too late.'

The officer did not grasp what Kerlon meant by this remark. But as soon as the magnifying screen clearly showed the three figures, he understood his commander's meaning.

The metal monster that was walking toward their ships was unmistakably an Arkonide robot.

And at the same time they could distinguish Khrest, who advanced, tall and straight with the inborn pride of his race, toward the waiting ships. Although he was dressed in some unfamiliar garb, rather than the usual uniform of the expeditionary forces of the Arkonide space fleet, his racial extraction was quite obvious. At his side strode a short stocky man with a colorful cape – whom Kerlon took to be a native of this planet.

'Too bad,' Kerlon murmured, evidently disappointed. 'And I thought our expedition was the first to have discovered this system. Someone else has beaten us to it. I wonder who it might be?'

'Shall we go out and meet them halfway?' asked the officer.

'It would be a friendly gesture,' Kerlon said and stood up. 'Switch off the screen and accompany me.'

It was a clear-cut case for Kerlon. One of the many expeditions that searched the universe for inhabited solar systems had landed on this planet and established contact with the natives. That was a completely normal procedure. Sooner or later this gigantic solar system would therefore become part of the galactic empire. It was too bad that he wouldn't be credited with this discovery. It was a regrettable fact but one that couldn't be changed.

'Shall we sound the alarm?' asked the officer. But he already knew the answer.

Kerlon shook his head. 'What for? It's quite obvious that we're dealing here, with friendly natives, otherwise the Arkonide and his robot wouldn't be able to move around unhindered. No, there's no danger.'

And Kerlon, accompanied by his officer, left the ship to meet Khrest and his companions.

Skillfully utilizing dips and furrows in the ground and seeking cover behind clumps of bushes had enabled Gagat and ten of his bravest warriors to steal up close to the three spaceships. The eleven men lay pressed close to the ground, hidden by the tall grass, waiting for further developments.

Then they saw three figures descend from the castle and make their way toward the ships. Soon two other men emerged from the mysterious silver ships and walked toward the other group. Barely twenty yards from Gagat's hiding place the two groups met and began to converse. Unfortunate, thought Gagat, that he could not understand a word they were saying.

'They know each other,' Gagat whispered. He was disappointed. 'They have come to conquer our world. Lesur is their ally. We must kill them.'

His new chieftain Radgar placed his right hand on Gagat's arm. He murmured with a raucous voice, 'Shouldn't we rather take them prisoners than kill them? Once they are in our power the other Gods won't dare attack us anymore.'

Gagat could see his point. 'You're very clever, Radgar,' he praised the man. 'They'll be no good to us if they're dead but they'll be very useful as hostages. Take care not to injure them. Wait for my signal, then we'll rush them. We must take them by surprise; they mustn't get a chance to defend themselves.'

And once more they pressed even closer to the earth, hoping that the strangers would come still nearer to their hiding place.

Khrest was not the least surprised when he saw the two Arkonides walk toward him. Still, it was hard for him to suppress a peculiar feeling.

The two men that came nearer and nearer had been dead these past ten thousand years. A vast chasm separated them, still they would confront each other presently. Death had been overcome; exercising some influence on future events had become possible too.

But was this truly the case? What he was about to do now, was this not an indispensable necessity in order to make possible what would happen in ten thousand years – or rather what already had taken place by now?

What, on the other hand, wondered Khrest, *would happen if I were not standing here this moment and if Kerlon and I would never meet?* And the answer came to him instantly: somebody else would be standing here in his place, advising Kerlon to fly off to Earth's solar system.

And then they finally confronted each other.

'I see,' Kerlon began with a slight smile, 'that my expedition has arrived too late. You've stolen a march on us.'

Khrest understood at once. He decided to play along. 'We've found this system quite by accident, Kerlon, and we believe it will be possible to incorporate it into our galactic empire. The natives, the Ferrons, are willing to become Arkonide subjects.'

And in the same instant Khrest realized that he had committed an important blunder. How could he have known Kerlon's name?

Kerlon raised his eyebrows. 'You know me? I can't remember ever having met you before.'

Khrest caught himself in time. 'I'm Khrest. My spaceship is off to another exploratory trip to the other planets of this system. A few of my crew and I have remained behind. The center on Arkon reported that you were on your way here.'

Kerlon shook his head. 'Strange,' he said. 'Nobody had any inkling of my intention to explore this system. It can be nothing but sheer guesswork on their part. It's only an accident that we are meeting here.'

'Since when are we permitted to carry out missions without special authorization?' Khrest questioned him in a chiding tone while trying to hide his own embarrassment. He knew that Kerlon would not dare make inquiries at the center on Arkon. It constituted an illegal act in itself to have come here without being ordered to do so.

'But be it as it may,' Khrest resumed, 'to be honest with you – I haven't informed the center about my exact location. They assume that I merely touched this sector in passing. Therefore you're fully entitled to claim the discovery of this system for yourself. I hope that you'll regard me with a little more sympathy from now on. . . .'

Kerlon exchanged astonished glances with his officer, then extended his hand in a friendly greeting. 'This is very kind of you, Khrest. You're right, it'll be wiser to conceal this meeting entirely from our center. And, quite frankly, it's most important for me to be officially known as the discoverer of this system. I have my reasons for it. Let me tell you, I'm on the track of a very great secret. Once this mystery is solved, it will bestow absolute power to our race over the entire universe.'

'If you're referring to the secret of eternal life, I can give you some additional clues,' Khrest said calmly.

Kerlon's eyes went wide with horror. What he had believed to be his own personal secret was mentioned here by this strange commander in an almost matter-of-fact tone of voice. Khrest realized that he must have gone a bit too far. How could he lessen the shock?

'I've found some clues that indicate the existence of a race in our universe that has discovered the secret of cell rejuvenation. I believe this is nonsense. But on the other hand I see that you take this whole story more seriously than I do. That's none of my business. Since I have no intention of following up this trail, let me tell you where I suppose the trail will lead next. There is a solar system some twenty-seven light-years distant. . . .'

'I know.' Kerlon nodded in agreement, quite to Khrest's surprise. 'This is where the trail leads. Thanks for your kindness, Khrest. As soon as I have registered my discovery of this system – and this is happening while we're talking, via the positronic brain – I shall proceed to the other solar system twenty-seven light-years from here. And how about you? What are your plans?'

Khrest smiled. 'I've been ordered to search sector AM Fifty-three Y. One of our space vessels is supposed to have crash-landed there.'

Khrest had arbitrarily picked these coordinates.

'Fine.' Kerlon nodded, satisfied. 'Then we've come to an agreement. Do you plan on leaving this planet as soon as your ship returns?'

'Yes.'

'How did you get along with the natives here?'

'There are various tribes. The inhabitants of the castle over there believe us to be Gods. They're devoted to us. We came to their assistance while they were being attacked by some enemies, the so-called barbarians.'

'You intervened in the internal affairs of an inferior race?' asked Kerlon, astonished.

'We were forced to defend ourselves,' Khrest replied.

'But it is forbidden to fight against primitive races.'

'Self-defense is allowed,' countered Khrest.

Kerlon was just about to say something but before he could utter a word a most startling event took place. This very moment Gagat decided to overwhelm these valuable hostages.

With Gagat in the lead, the band of warriors rushed toward Khrest's and Kerlon's groups who were quickly surrounded. At the sight of the barbarians' raised swords Khrest deemed it wise not to draw the ray gun that was hanging at his belt. They were completely taken by surprise. No defense was possible without endangering their own lives.

Even Markon the robot recognized the danger of their situation. He realized that any counterattack would only aggravate their risky position. If he were to engage the barbarians in battle, one of them would certainly find some opportunity to kill either Khrest or Lesur. Therefore the robot remained inactive. There was no threat to his own survival at any time, whichever way he would act, but his creators' lives had to be protected at all costs. Even if it would have meant his own destruction, he would always have considered first his masters' welfare.

Gagat touched the tip of his sword to Lesur's chest. 'Even your Gods can't help you now!' he reminded him sarcastically. 'But never fear, we won't harm you and your friends. As soon as they hand over their silver spheres to me, those giant flying vessels, I will let them go free.'

Khrest understood his words, while Kerlon naturally could not make any sense of them. He had some vague idea what the barbarians might have in mind, however as they gestured toward the spheres. Still, he could not imagine what use the barbarians could possibly make of the spaceships once they were in their possession.

'I'm warning you.' Lesur spoke up bravely, although he had never felt so close to death as at that moment, 'Our Gods can destroy you if they so desire. The reason they've shown you mercy is to give you another chance. Let us go free or you'll bitterly regret it.'

Kerlon had given up any hope. Surely his crew had observed this incident from the safety of the spaceships, but how could they come to their commander's assistance without definitely endangering his and his officer's life even more? Besides, there was the ban on using deadly weapons against primitive peoples.

Derisive laughter was Gagat's answer to Lesur's warning. He brandished his sword and motioned to his men. 'Two of you walk on either side of each prisoner. Make sure you can kill them at any moment, if necessary. Watch out, they're full of tricks. We must take them back to our camps where we can lock them up securely.'

Kerlon looked at Khrest, and not without blame he reminded him: 'It appears you hadn't sufficient opportunity to make a thorough study of these natives' customs. Otherwise this incident couldn't have occurred.'

'Don't worry, Kerlon,' Khrest comforted the other Arkonide. 'It won't be long before we'll be free again. My friends are already aware of what has taken place here and will act at any moment now. They're probably only waiting for the most favorable occasion. But once they start their action to liberate us, please, do me the favor not to be surprised at anything. Don't ask any questions, will you?'

'What's that supposed to mean?'

'Keep quiet now. The barbarians will become suspicious otherwise. Just this: my friends keep in constant communication with me. They can even hear what we're saying. They'll intervene very soon. I only hope that your crew in the spaceships will remain calm.'

'If they should disregard the ban and try to set me free, I wouldn't really blame them.'

'Of course not. But look here, Kerlon! Our captivity has already come to an end. I must insist, though, don't ask me for any explanation!'

This reminder was necessary for in Kerlon's eyes the ensuing events must have seemed more than improbable. It must all be a wild dream!

Gagat's sword suddenly took on a life of its own. It slipped out of his hand and rose slowly upward. About five yards above their heads the weapon hung in the air without moving. The barbarians were thunderstruck at this sight. They forgot all about their leader's command. They no longer even worried that they themselves might be taken prisoner by their former captives. They stared up at the hovering sword that quickly was joined by nine more. Defying gravity, the heavy weapons climbed skyward, arranged in an orderly, structured ornament. Then the tips of all ten swords began to point to the center and formed a perfect circle. There was only one gap where the eleventh sword had not yet taken its place. Its owner was not willing to surrender his weapon so easily, despite all this frightening magic. Desperately clutching his sword, the barbarian would not let go of it.

But Anne Sloane's telekinetic abilities were stronger.

She directed the weapon higher and higher. The sword kept rising, pulling the desperately struggling barbarian after it.

The brave warrior wildly kicked his legs, trying to regain the ground with his feet. In vain! He was hanging almost three yards above the grass by now. Unrelenting, the sword dragged him up into the air. Finally the barbarian seemed to realize that it would be useless to keep resisting the will of the Gods.

He let go of the sword and fell back to the ground. Anne did not bother to break his fall. She had all she could manage to hold the beautiful arrangement of the swords intact way above the group's heads.

The barbarians were disarmed.

Calmly Khrest drew his ray gun and pointed it at Gagat.

'You see how senseless it is for you to try to rebel. And now, run for your lives! The next time I might not be as patient and merciful!'

Gagat looked longingly once more at the inaccessible swords. Then, remembering the most unpleasant effect of the odd weapon held in the hand of the white-haired superman, he followed the stranger's advice. With

Gagat in the lead, the barbarians retreated to the nearby woods.

Kerlon hardly paid attention to the withdrawing barbarians, he was too busy staring at the eleven floating swords. He was absolutely fascinated and utterly perplexed.

Khrest felt it was time to offer some kind of explanation to Kerlon. 'I told you earlier, Kerlon, not to be surprised at anything. You might also have noticed that the mysterious happenings made no particular impression on the primitives. Despite its backwardness, this planet has produced many things we're not too familiar with. What you just witnessed here was the work of a telekineticist.'

'I thought so. Do you know him?'

'Yes. A Ferron whose brain is way ahead of his time. There are entire races of telekineticists. Our scientific research—'

'I know,' Kerlon interrupted with resignation in his voice. 'We'll never completely understand this phenomenon, unfortunately. In any case, this fellow has saved us from a dangerous situation and we owe him our thanks.'

'The best way to express our gratitude would be to forget the whole incident.' Khrest spoke with emphasis. 'The Ferronian natives believe that we've endowed this man with this special talent. They might get suspicious if we start making a great to-do about it.'

This seemed to make sense to Kerlon. But he still couldn't take his eyes off the sword circle in the air. Then, pointing to his waiting ships, he invited Khrest to come aboard for a visit.

Khrest accepted. But he still had no idea what Kerlon would have to give him in order to find the way to the light.

6. THE BLACK GHOST

Meanwhile Rhodan was facing a difficult decision.

'The last message indicated not to wait more than three days before returning to the time-transformer. Today is the third day since our arrival here. But this means a Ferronian day, because by Earth time three days have already gone by.'

Bell became quite jittery. 'What if we wrongly interpreted this message and the immortals really meant to say three Terrestrial days?'

'Then we'd be stuck here,' Rhodan admitted undisturbed. 'But I'm convinced that the immortal always reckons according to the time of the planet where the particular task is to be solved by us. This means we still have time until this afternoon. Marshall, what's going on with Khrest's group?'

The telepath sat in a corner of the room, quietly concentrating. 'Khrest and Lesur are accompanying Kerlon into the flagship of the expedition. Markon is waiting outside. Kerlon was just telling Khrest that he wished to show him something.'

'Hurray!' chortled Bell. 'That's it!'

'That's what?'

'The thing we're after, what else! The path to the light. Couldn't Ralf Marten get into the action? He's just sitting around twiddling his thumbs. He looks bored.'

The slant-eyed mutant smiled. 'Bored? That would be exaggerating. But it wouldn't be a bad idea if I could take over Kerlon for a while. He won't notice anything. Marshall can read my thoughts and report to you whatever I'm seeing and hearing. For this purpose I'll leave behind in my body here a small part of my conscious mind. With the other part I shall control Kerlon. He'll be totally unaware that I'm spying this way and we'll get a splendid view of what's going on over there in the Arkonide flagship.'

Rhodan liked the idea. 'Yes, and I also prefer not to leave the two Arkonides alone by themselves. After all, they are compatriots.'

'Don't you trust Khrest?' Bell said. 'He won't risk anything foolish.'

'Not intentionally, Reg. But even our Arkonide supermen are not infallible, as we unfortunately have found at times. We must be ready to intervene at any moment if necessary. Just imagine what would have happened if Anne Sloane hadn't chased away those barbarians.'

'That was easy for her, as long as she could see the scene from the castle watch tower. But she cannot operate inside the spaceships — she can't see through the metal hull. We must be doubly alert, I admit. All right then, Marten, give up your ghost!'

Marten stretched out on a couch and shortly fell into a trance. Marshall rested next to him, constantly probing his friend's mind as he perceived all that Kerlon was saying and hearing. The teleoptician had taken over Kerlon's senses and now shared all his impressions.

'Khrest and Lesur are sitting at a table together with Kerlon and his officer,' the telepath reported in a monotonous voice. 'Kerlon is telling something about a pyramid. Yes, he's talking about the pyramid he discovered somewhere on Ferrol. In the mountains. And inside the pyramid there was a matter transmitter. He says he expressed his amazement when he saw it there. And he found something else there – a metal cylinder. He wants to show it to Khrest.'

Rhodan glanced at his friend Bell. 'I believe you were right. That's it!' Bell grinned and contently nodded his head in silent triumph.

John Marshall continued: 'Kerlon says he has so far tried in vain to open that cylinder. Khrest wants to hold the tube in his hand. Kerlon refuses to let him do so. He insists the tube belongs to him. Besides, it might be dangerous for Khrest to touch this mysterious object. One can never know what dangers these unknown worlds might harbor. They've just seen proof of such an inexplicable phenomenon. Khrest pretends now not to be interested in the tube. That's a clever ruse, for now Kerlon feels cheated. He wanted to impress Khrest and brag about this sensational find. He says this cylinder is somehow connected with the race of the immortals that's living somewhere in this sector of the universe. Khrest pretends that this is most improbable. He's carrying his role off splendidly!'

Marshall fell silent. Marten lay motionless. The room became completely quiet. The silence was broken by Anne Sloane, who returned to the room from the watch tower.

'I've let the swords fall from high up onto the bare

rocks down below. They're pretty useless now, I guess.'

Rhodan raised a finger to his lips, motioning Anne to sit down quietly. She took a seat next to Ras Tschubai, who was impatiently waiting his turn.

Marshall resumed his report of what Ralf Marten was seeing through Kerlon's eyes.

'An officer enters the cabin where the four men are sitting. The crew had observed some natives who are creeping toward the ships. It looks as if an attack is imminent. According to the officer's description, the group seems to be barbarians. Kerlon is bound by his Arkonide code. He's not permitted to engage in a fight with them. Khrest insists on leaving the ship at once. Lesur seems desperate. He's afraid to leave this refuge; he feels safe inside the spaceship. Khrest gets up, hesitates. The metal capsule! How can he bring it into his possession? Kerlon appears to notice his sudden interest. He smiles and pushes the roll into his belt, believing it to be safe there. Then he offers to accompany his guests to the entrance hatch.'

Rhodan quickly glanced at Anne. 'Are the spaceships clearly visible from the watch tower?'

Anne nodded affirmatively. 'Excellent view. I can make out Markon without any difficulty. He's standing below the entrance hatch of the middle ship.'

'Splendid! Ras, you'll come with us. Anne, you too. Marshall, stay here and listen to what else Marten will have to report. Let's hurry! Come along, Reg!'

They rushed past a few astonished Ferrons and ran up the many stairs that led to the platform and onto the watch tower. From high up there the view was magnificent, as Anne had said. It stretched beyond the plain, to the woods as far as the distant mountain range. Three giant spaceships were poised on the plain. From the nearby woods a horde of barbarians emerged, storming toward the spaceships almost half a mile away. Gagat raced at the head of nearly one hundred warriors. He no longer bothered to camouflage his movements. This was his last desperate attempt. Quite openly he proceeded to attack the spaceships with spears and swords. The leniency the God had shown so far he interpreted as weakness. Gagat felt optimistic.

Khrest and Lesur left the ship. Kerlon was standing above them in the open hatch. The silvery cylinder was plainly visible, tucked in his belt. He was waving a farewell greeting, evidently not caring about Khrest's safety. After all, Khrest had insisted on leaving. Perhaps Kerlon was secretly hoping that the witness of his presumed defeat would even vanish for good.

But that was nonsense. Khrest had assured him he would not claim any discovery rights of this planet. Whatever the reason, Kerlon was curious enough to wait a while longer before the takeoff. He wanted to see how Khrest would extricate himself from this precarious situation.

As soon as Khrest and his companion reached Markon, the three began to move in the direction of the castle. Gagat was wise enough to refrain from attacking the small group. He knew from bitter experience that it would be useless. Gagat's goal was the ships, nothing else.

Khrest knew that his mission had failed. He had seen the cylinder and intuited that this was the mysterious something he was supposed to bring back from the past. Should he have wrested it by force from Kerlon's hands? What would have happened if Kerlon's suspicions had been aroused? Would he ever have flown on to Earth's solar system?

Now it was Rhodan's turn to intervene. This was the last resort.

Kerlon followed the small group with his eyes. He began to realize the oddity of this encounter. Who was that man who knew so much and yet asked so many questions? Why did he voluntarily renounce recognition as the official discoverer of this inhabited solar system? What information did he have about that race, totally unknown and unheard of by everyone else?

Questions, questions, but no answers.

Kerlon wondered why the barbarians so obviously ignored Khrest, Lesur and the robot. Unmolested, the three marched toward the castle. Meanwhile the barbarians raced toward the spaceships, brandishing their swords and spears, yelling lustily.

Kerlon turned abruptly to enter the airlock. He stumbled and for a moment lost his footing. He caught himself in time by grasping the frame of the airlock with his hands. This sudden movement loosened his belt for a second. The smooth metal cylinder slipped out, dropping straight down to the thick grass below the entrance.

Kerlon saw how the cylinder fell into a small crevice in the ground and rolled over to the side.

He hesitated. The cylinder was part of the trail he was pursuing. He had to get it back. On the other hand, the barbarians had come quite close and began to hurl their primitive weapons against him. And he was not permitted to defend himself nor to use force against them. This was the unalterable law! Little did he know that just a few centuries later this law would be overturned.

He shouted a command. Seconds later the other two spaceships lifted off, slowly rising into the sky. The flagship still remained on the ground. Its heat cannons began to spew flames.

The barbarians were horrified. A fiery circle was drawn in front of them. The circle drew closer and closer. A heat wave seemed to sear their lungs; smoke choked their breath. The grass started to burn. The smoke drifted upward. The barbarians hesitated. They stopped the attack which had seemed to be going in their favor.

Kerlon activated the escalator. He slid down into the middle of the protective ring of fire his guns had placed. He was safe inside. No native would dare penetrate this wall of flames. He must retrieve the metal cylinder.

He began to search in the grass, trying to locate the small crevice into which the metal cylinder had rolled. It had to be close by. He looked here and there, ignoring the few poorly aimed spears that came flying through the curtain of smoke.

At the very moment he spotted the tube lying a couple of feet away, something weird and terrifying occurred.

A dark shape materialized in the midst of the smoke. The ghost wore a uniform but his face, bare arms and hands were black.

Kerlon was frightened out of his wits although he was not the least bit superstitious.

Before Kerlon could even make a move, the black figure bent over and picked the cylinder off the ground. And while Kerlon watched helplessly, Ras Tschubai dissolved again into the air and disappeared.

And with him, as Kerlon noted with impotent rage, vanished his precious, indispensable metal cylinder.

A spear whizzed by close to his head and he realized that he was in immediate danger. Hastily he jumped onto the upward rolling escalator and rose up to the entrance hatch. He was filled with searing fury at Khrest, the black ghost and everything living on this planet.

But he had to abide by his nation's laws.

He issued commands for immediate takeoff and followed the other two spacespheres that were waiting for him in the upper layers of the atmosphere.

They touched down again on another region of Ferrol and stayed there for three days. Then they left the planet for good.

Without ever stopping they cruised about the system, passed dead and uninhabited planets until they reached the empty space beyond the forty-third planet. Then Kerlon ordered a transition maneuver. His destination was a solar system more than twenty-seven light-years away, whose third planet showed the beginning signs of a primitive race trying to free itself from the shackles of ignorance and backwardness.

The forefathers of those who eventually would build the Tower of Babel were about to be born.

7. IMMORTALITY – OR – FATALITY?

Rhodan examined the metal cylinder with a puzzled expression.

Bell made his usual unsolicited comments. 'Looks like a specimen drum the bug catchers use way back home on Earth. I wonder what's inside.'

'One of the many answers we need for solving the galactic riddle – a small step ahead on the endless trail leading to eternity. But we can't waste any time now on idle speculations. Our time here will be up soon.'

They had taken leave of Lesur and his followers and had returned to the empty vaulted chamber underneath the castle. The metal cube was lying untouched and unchanged in the center of the room. Nothing about the cube gave any indication whether they were still in the past or had already returned to present time. Their only clue lay in the size of the hall itself. It had grown larger upon their arrival. Therefore it would most likely contract to its former proportions once they started on their return trip to the future.

Rhodan glanced at his watch. 'Our three days have come to an end. It's just a matter of minutes now, and then . . .'

He stopped in midsentence and listened. Somewhere in the wide corridors outside the wooden door he heard a man scream, long and loud. Then came the clanging of swords in battle. Seconds later, the noise of heavy fighting right outside the heavy door of the underground chamber.

Ras Tschubai looked at Rhodan, a question in his dark eyes. Bell quickly glanced at the metal cube and said: 'The barbarians! They're attacking the castle again! All our efforts to help Ferrol were in vain.'

'We can't know in advance what fate has in store,' Rhodan said slowly. 'Fate apparently didn't plan for Lesur and his people to win this fight. It's too late now to come to his rescue once more.'

Before Bell could reply, heavy blows, thudded against the door that separated them from the basement of the castle. Excited voices and shrill commands could be heard. Then sudden silence. A deep voice said a few words which were followed by triumphant shouts. Some men apparently ran out of the room, then their returning steps became audible again to the eager listeners inside the secret chamber. Now they seemed to place some objects directly in front of the door. Some men laughed raucously and expectantly.

Rhodan turned to Ras Tschubai. 'Have a look at what they're planning to do. Be careful and return right away.'

Ras vanished before Rhodan had hardly finished speaking.

Five seconds later he rematerialized. Rhodan noticed at once a bleeding wound on the African's neck.

'They plan to blow up the door,' Ras panted, pressing his hand against his injured neck. 'They must have found some blasting powder here at the castle. One of the barbarians had the presence of mind to throw his sword at me. It's just a slight cut. We must get away from here immediately or we'll be lost.'

'I wish we could vanish,' Bell lamented in a furious voice. 'Unless this time-transformer functions to save us, we'll all be blown to bits and pieces. Even if we did get this beautiful metal cylinder!'

Rhodan looked again at his watch. 'Our time is up now. Either now – or never.' He turned to Khrest. 'How can the immortal know that we've solved our task? He exists in present time, or do you think he traveled backward in time with us?'

Khrest had no chance to reply for the robot spoke up: 'He didn't accompany us, only his spirit did – in the time-transformer. Place the cylinder on the time-transformer, then the positronic brain will check whether it's the object we were supposed to retrieve from the past.'

Silently Rhodan carried out Markon's instructions.

Meanwhile all had become quiet outside the chamber door. The barbarians apparently had withdrawn. Was the fuse already burning?

'Ras, go, and extinguish the fuse!'

Ras, whose wound had meanwhile been dressed by Anne Sloane, unhesitatingly obeyed Rhodan's command although he full well realized he risked being left behind in the past in case the secret chamber should be suddenly transported ahead to the future.

Ras was back again within three seconds. 'Impossible, I can't do anything out there!' he shouted, his eyes dilated in terror. 'There's no fuse. They simply spread loose powder all over the place outside the door. I imagine they'll ignite the powder by shooting a burning arrow into that mess from a safe distance. There's nothing I can do to prevent that.'

'Then the archer will have to be . . .' began Khrest but he was interrupted by the sudden hum of the time-transformer. It had started to function again. The floor beneath their feet was vibrating. Slowly the cellar shrank in size. The walls were smooth again.

The return journey to the future had begun. And none too soon. While the wooden door disappeared and gave way to a smooth metal wall, the time travelers were thrown to the ground by a tremendous shockwave. A bright flash of light blinded them momentarily. They barely felt the sudden heat wave. At the same time it grew almost dark again inside the room.

'We're on our way,' Rhodan said, relieved, but sounding quite matter-of-fact, as if time traveling were an everyday occurrence. 'I'm confident we've made it.'

'Everyone except me has contributed their share to the success of this mission,' Dr Haggard complained. 'Why did you want me along, then?'

Rhodan smiled. 'We're all very happy that we didn't need your services, Doc. But you didn't make the trip totally unneeded. Take care of Ras. Anne Sloane's handkerchief is drenched with blood.'

Stepping out of the transmitter that had brought them back to the base on Ferrol, they saw Thora.

The beautiful Arkonide woman grew pale at the sight of Rhodan, Khrest and the rest of the group. Unmistakable disappointment showed in her face. But when she discovered a three days' growth of beard on the men's faces her disappointment rapidly changed to astonishment.

Slowly she approached the group and looked at the metal cylinder Rhodan held in his hands. She could barely move her lips as she inquired, 'I don't quite understand – where did you get this?'

'From Kerlon,' replied Rhodan. 'Why should it startle you so much? Wasn't this the purpose of our trip?'

'How could I possibly have forgotten – in such a short while!'

She emphasized the last five words in a peculiar manner as she again scanned the men's faces, her eyes questioning and puzzled. Khrest understood at once what her problem was. The immortal was fond of playing tricks on mere mortal creatures. This was not the first time he had done so. Distorting time was nothing but a game and still another means of bluffing and leading astray those who were voluntarily pursuing the trail he had placed for them.

Khrest's face was hairless. Bell, however, rubbed his stubbly beard and grumbled in embarrassment: 'What do you mean by such a short while? Three days will do that to any grown man on Earth.'

'How long were we gone?' asked Khrest.

'Exactly half an hour,' Thora answered softly.

'I believe,' Rhodan remarked in a matter-of-fact voice, 'we'll have to get used to such things as long as we're dealing with a being that has mastered time and the five dimensions. I often try to imagine what he might look like but I haven't arrived at any conclusion yet.'

To the surprise of everyone, Markon joined the conversation without having been invited to do so.

'The immortal doesn't look like anything at all. . . .'

Once again Rhodan was sitting in the center of the positronic brain.

It had been an easy task to open the metal cylinder. The automatic seal of the lid had sprung open the moment they arrived in the present time. The lid had simply been sealed by a time lock.

Inside the tube was a thin foil covered with glowing symbols. Rhodan made a photocopy before he inserted the original into the intake slot of the positronic brain. Then the loudspeaker announced:

THIS MESSAGE IS NOT WRITTEN IN CODE. TRANSLATION FOLLOWS SHORTLY. WRITTEN VERSION WILL BE AVAILABLE IN HALF AN HOUR.

That had been twenty minutes ago.

Khrest, Bell, Haggard and Thora were waiting together with Rhodan.

'We must realize,' began Rhodan, 'that the tasks are becoming increasingly more difficult. The immortal becomes more and more demanding and less considerate of our safety at the same time. If we get caught in a deadly trap it'll be up to us to set ourselves free again. If we should die while trying . . .' Rhodan shrugged his shoulders.

'The trail is getting more complex and difficult to follow,' agreed Khrest. Then he continued: 'The track has been placed in such a way, though, that those endowed with superior intelligence and special talents cannot lose it. But if the pursuers should lack the necessary qualifications, they're doomed to perish. And if they lose their lives during the search they don't deserve the gift of immortality. Our unknown friend has everything carefully calculated.'

Rhodan looked at Khrest. 'I'm confident the next step will be more challenging than those before.'

'We can count on that for sure. But this will also mean that we've come a bit nearer our goal. That will be a reward in itself.'

'And the next time,' remarked Thora, 'I shall join you. I'm entitled to participate in this quest.'

Their conversation was interrupted by a loud hum from the brain. The paper strip with the announced translation emerged from the answer slot. Bell, who was nearest, picked it up and read it aloud:

WHOEVER WISHES TO FIND THE WAY MAY STILL TURN BACK. BUT IF HE DECIDES TO PURSUE THE TRAIL, HE MAY REST ASSURED THAT HE WILL NO LONGER RECEIVE ANY ASSISTANCE. SOON THE UNIVERSE WILL BE SHAKEN. INVESTIGATE, BUT CONSIDER THAT THIS WORLD IS ALIEN AND GIGANTIC.

Bell's face was one big question mark as he looked at Rhodan. 'How do you like that? It sounds like another of his riddles.'

Rhodan did not reply. He sat with eyes half-closed.

Khrest took the message from Bell and carefully read the text several times before he passed it on to Thora. She too tried to fathom the meaning of the baffling message.

Bell spoke impatiently. 'The universe will be shaken, according to the message. That's what we're supposed to wait for? What mysterious thing is going to send a shockwave through space – maybe an atomic explosion?' To make each point he punctuated his sentences by a bang of his fist on the table.

'Not necessarily,' said Khrest. 'The transition of a large spaceship is enough to cause such a shockwave throughout the universe. Perhaps a spaceship will arrive. What must we make, though, of the alien and gigantic world? It doesn't seem to me that Ferrol can be meant by that.'

Thora no longer seemed as confident as a short while before when she had insisted on participating in the solution of the next task. She expressed the doubts the message had engendered in her mind.

'My intuition tells me, Khrest, that no good will come of all this. There's danger ahead. We've been too arrogant and presumptuous. So far we've been lucky – extremely lucky. What if our good luck runs out?'

Rhodan opened his eyes and regarded Thora. His face was serious but not desperate. He was still leliberating.

Haggard ventured an opinion: 'Without hope life becomes meaningless. I'm against abandoning our search. What do you think, Rhodan?'

The Peacelord slowly lowered his head in contemplation. To all present an eternity seemed to pass till, resolutely, he looked up again. A steely glint plainly shone forth from his eyes. In that moment Earthmen and Arkonides knew beyond the shadow of a doubt that the search for the planet of eternal life would be – continued.

They would traverse the path ahead of them; accepting every challenge put before them, daring every danger, coping with every peril they would confront; pursuing the prize of life everlasting that glittered at the end of the quest.

What lay at the ultimate end – the deathly deception of a cruel alien Lorelei or the heady draft of immortality of a cosmic de Leon?

Siren fatality or Fountain of Youth?

Who could say for certain?

Rhodan's voice interrupted the reveries. 'No use racking our brains over what was meant by "the shaking of the universe". We'll find out in due time. But there *is* something that worries me – you know what I'm alluding to?'

Bell leaned forward and asked: 'No. What, Perry?'

'The message from the Unknown tells us that soon the universe will be shaken. *But when were these words recorded?* Ten thousand years ago? Earlier still? I am seriously wondering, what does an immortal being understand by "soon"?'

No one, of course, could venture a guess. Silence was the only answer.

'Soon' could mean tomorrow.

But it could also mean another thousand years!